When wishes don't come true . . .

Chrissie's father rose to his feet. 'Come on outside, Chrissie. Something very special is waiting for you.'

Her horse was waiting for her! Chrissie couldn't believe that after all the years she'd spent waiting, the big moment was finally here.

I've got to be the luckiest person in the world, Chrissie thought as she and her family walked toward the corral in what seemed like slow motion. *It just doesn't get better than this.*

But when Chrissie got to the gate of the corral, she froze. In the corral stood a gangly, gawky colt with a big red bow tied around his neck. His legs were way too long for his body, and he looked unsure on his feet. He stepped sideways, as if he was trying to steady himself, then tripped and almost fell. Watching him struggle to remain standing was more than Chrissie could bear.

'Where – where's Outstanding?' Chrissie finally stammered. 'Where is he?' She looked around wildly, turning in a circle, searching for her favourite foal. But it was useless. Outstanding wasn't there.

Cover illustration by Fred

MY FAVOURITE COLT

MALLORY STEVENS

KNIGHT BOOKS
Hodder and Stoughton

Published by arrangement with HarperCollins Publishers Inc
10 East 53rd Street, New York NY 10022-5299 USA
Produced by Daniel Weiss Associates Inc,
33 West 17th Street New York NY 10011

First published in Great Britain
by Hodder and Stoughton, 1994

10 9 8 7 6 5 4 3 2 1

British Library Cataloguing in Publication Data
A catalogue record for this book is available from
the British Library

ISBN 0 340 60839 0

Typeset by Avon Dataset Ltd, Bidford-on-Avon

Printed and bound in Great Britain by
Cox & Wyman Ltd, Reading, Berkshire

Hodder and Stoughton Ltd
A Division of Hodder Headline PLC
338 Euston Road
London NW1 3BH

One

CHRISSIE THREW OPEN THE BARN DOOR, AND THE smells of wet hay and horse rushed out to meet the fresh, cold air outside. She took a deep breath and felt her early-morning drowsiness fade instantly.

'Good morning, ladies,' Chrissie called out to the mares as she walked down the barn aisle.

A few of the horses whinnied in greeting, and others stirred in their stalls as they woke up from a night's sleep. Chrissie smiled contentedly. She had grown up around horses, and she couldn't imagine what life would be like without them.

Chrissie stopped at one of the stalls and poked her head in. 'Morning, Excellence,' she said. 'How are you and the baby doing today?' The very pregnant black Thoroughbred waddled

1

over to the stall door, and Chrissie reached out to rub her neck.

'Did you sleep well?' she said, keeping her voice low and steady so that the horse would feel at ease. The mare whickered and butted Chrissie with her nose playfully.

Chrissie laughed. Then she thought she saw something move in Excellence's swollen belly. *Could that be her foal?* Chrissie wondered as she leaned over to take a closer look. The mare's belly moved again, and Chrissie jumped back, a squeal of delight rising in her throat. She quickly cupped a hand over her mouth. She didn't want to frighten Excellence. The last thing she wanted to do was betray the trust that existed between her and her favourite horse.

The mare took a step forward and nuzzled up to Chrissie. 'You want some sugar, don't you?' Chrissie asked. She reached into her pocket and pulled out a couple of sugar cubes. After positioning the cubes in the centre of her open palm, she stretched out her arm and allowed the mare to lip up the sugar.

'Yuck,' Chrissie said, feeling something wet collect in her palm. She looked at the greenish horse slobber and wiped it on her jeans. 'That's really gross, Excellence,' she said with a disgusted look on her face. But she didn't *really* mind. Nothing about horses actually bothered Chrissie. In fact, sometimes she thought she liked horses more than she liked people.

'Well, I'd better go get some breakfast before I starve to death,' she said to the horse. 'But I'll come back and visit later.' She gave Excellence one last scratch between the ears before walking back down the aisle towards the barn door.

Chrissie stepped outside into the crisp winter air. The first snow of the season had fallen more than three weeks ago, and there were still several inches left. The sun reflected off the blanket of whiteness that covered Williams Farm, and Chrissie had to squint to see the thirty acres of rolling hills and lush meadows that made up the Williams Farm. It had been a dairy farm about a hundred years before, when Chrissie's great-grandparents had bought the land, but after a disease had killed all the cattle, her great-grandfather decided to begin raising horses. By the time Chrissie's father took over the business, Williams Farm was known throughout the country as one of the top breeders of Thoroughbred show horses.

Chrissie's stomach rumbled loudly as she made her way up the path to the house. She ran up the steps to the back door and burst into the kitchen, where her father and her brother, David, were already eating.

'Morning,' Chrissie said as she slid into her seat. 'I just went to see Excellence. She's *huge*. It looks like she's going to foal any minute now!'

David raised an eyebrow. 'Hey, can we hold off talking business till later, shrimp? I'm busy eating my breakfast,' he said playfully.

'It looks like you're trying to eat everyone else's breakfast, too,' Chrissie shot back. 'You think you can leave some for me?'

Chrissie and her seventeen-year-old brother constantly teased each other. At six feet, David was nearly as tall as their father, and he loved to make fun of Chrissie's petite size. He had straight blond hair and blue eyes, just like their mother, but he also had a rugged quality that seemed to drive girls crazy.

'You got it,' David answered with a wide grin. 'After all, you do need to eat as much as you can so that one day you'll be able to look Excellence in the eye.'

'That's enough, you two,' Mr. Williams said, jumping in before Chrissie had a chance to lunge across the table. 'Save your energy for the work that needs to be done at the barn.'

Chrissie's father sounded slightly gruffer than usual, but she knew he had been on edge lately. Excellence was the farm's best mare, so it wasn't surprising that he was a little nervous about the birth of her new foal. Mr. Williams had bought the sleek black Thoroughbred as a filly at the annual yearling auction ten years earlier, and every foal she'd had since had gone on to become a champion. So Excellence was in constant demand by breeders nationwide, and her foals commanded top prices.

Now the mare was heading into the last month of pregnancy, and everyone was anxiously awaiting the new foal – especially Chrissie. She loved Excellence more than any other horse on the farm, and she secretly hoped that her parents would give her the responsibility of raising the mare's foal. She knew she'd be perfect for the job. And her parents were going to entrust her with one of the farm's foals soon anyway, in just two months, when Chrissie turned thirteen.

The Williamses had a family tradition where every child, upon reaching the age of thirteen, was given a newborn foal to raise in preparation for the yearling auction in December. Chrissie's father had been the first Williams to be given a foal to raise, and he still talked about how thrilled he had been the day he turned thirteen. He had told Chrissie and David many stories about how clever and sweet his filly had been, and Chrissie knew he had been sad when it came time to sell her. But afterwards, his father had given him more responsibilities around the farm, and he began receiving a salary instead of an allowance. Also, because he had successfully raised the horse by himself, his father began to treat him like an adult.

When David turned thirteen, he had carried

on the tradition by raising a colt named Gallant Boy, and Chrissie remembered how he used to spend hours and hours with his horse. The colt had been sold at the end of that year, and David, too, had begun receiving a salary. He also got to keep half of what Gallant Boy sold for, and every year after that, Mr. Williams had let him raise other foals.

Soon it would be Chrissie's turn. She knew she was ready to take on the responsibility of raising her own horse. She had always enjoyed helping out with the horses, and she was good at it. Now she would have full charge of her very own horse, and Chrissie had a feeling that her father would give her the one she wanted most to raise – Excellence's foal. He *knew* how much she loved the Thoroughbred mare.

Chrissie was sure that the foal would be beautiful. Excellence was sleek and graceful, and Warrior, the sire, was tall and had nearly perfect conformation. By the end of the year, the foal would sell for a lot of money, and with half the profits, Chrissie could finally buy a good show-jumping horse.

She would have to wait a whole year to buy a show jumper, but for now she was thrilled at the idea of working with the horses. Caring for her foal would be only a small part of her responsibilities. She would also have to help clean the stables and barns, exercise the horses, feed and water them, and do other chores. And like David, she would be paid the same hourly wages as the hired hands.

Chrissie already received a generous allowance for helping her mum around the house and assisting her father with some of the simpler tasks around the stables, like cleaning tack and mucking out stalls. But the idea of getting real pay and her own responsibilities made her wish that her thirteenth birthday was that day.

'Bob, dear, don't forget that the vet is coming by around ten to check on the pregnant mares. She's also going to do a final check on the yearlings before they go to auction,' Melinda Williams said to her husband as she set a plate of eggs on the table.

In addition to Excellence, more than a dozen other mares at the farm were in their last month or so of pregnancy, and Chrissie knew that meant the Williamses were heading into a very busy season.

Chrissie always looked forward to this time of year. Receiving Christmas presents in December was nothing compared to the excitement of watching new foals being born in January.

'Okay, honey,' he said as he kissed his wife on the cheek. 'I'm going to take her over to check on Excellence as soon as she comes. We can't take any chances with that mare,' he said with a little frown.

Chrissie looked from her mother to her father, then took a deep breath. 'Uh, Dad,' she began, 'can I come along with you and Dr. Anderson? I'm almost finished with all my chores, and Excellence really likes me. I could even help out with her until her foal comes.'

'Of course you can come along and watch, but that's all,' her father replied. 'We've got grooms to take care of her, so there's no need for you to get involved with all of that.'

Mrs. Williams spoke up before Chrissie had a chance to protest. 'Chrissie, we've been through this before. You don't have enough experience with pregnant mares to care for Excellence.'

'Mum, I know how to take care of horses. And I'm sure I can handle Excellence even if she is pregnant.'

Her father smiled at her. 'Chrissie, it's not that we don't trust you. There's just no reason to take chances with you or Excellence. Her condition is very delicate now, you know.' He put down his fork and sat back, crossing his arms over his broad chest. 'Be patient. I promise you, you'll have your hands full soon enough with your own foal.'

Chrissie grinned at her father. Did he realise how much raising a foal meant to her? And to care for Excellence's foal . . . that would be like a dream come true.

'Don't worry. I'm ready,' Chrissie said, her heart swelling with pride. 'You don't know how ready I am.'

David laughed, but Chrissie didn't care if he thought she was silly. She wanted her father to know how much the horses meant to her, and she wanted to let him know that she could handle anything – even Excellence's foal.

'Believe me, Chrissie, I understand,' her father said as he rose from his chair and carried a stack of dishes to the sink. 'I was thirteen once, too.'

Chrissie watched her dad run some water over the dishes. He was a gentle-looking man despite his height – six-two – and he had curly brown hair that was just beginning to turn grey at the temples. He sometimes joked that Chrissie was responsible for his grey hair. He spent a lot of time outdoors, so his face was slightly weathered, and he was always tanned, winter or summer.

By contrast, Chrissie's mother looked younger than her age. In fact, she hadn't changed much since her college days. Chrissie had seen pictures of her in an old yearbook, and her mother had had the same short blonde hair and youthful face that she had now.

'Chrissie,' her mother said from across the

table, 'why don't you come to the shops with me after we've cleaned up? We should try to finish up our Christmas shopping today, because we may not have another chance once we start getting ready for the yearling auction.'

Chrissie, who'd been slipping scraps of food under the table to their dog, an Australian shepherd named King, looked from her mother to her father before answering.

'I'd rather watch Doc Anderson work with Excellence. We can go shopping another time, can't we?' she said.

'We don't have much more free time before the holidays – the auction is in less than two weeks, and Christmas is just a few days after that,' her mother said. 'Don't worry, Chrissie. I think Excellence will be just fine for a couple of hours without you.'

Chrissie looked down at her plate, disappointed. 'All right. But I'd like to get back early so I can spend some time with the horses, okay?'

'Okay,' her mother agreed.

Then suddenly Chrissie had an idea. 'Mum, can I call Debbie to see if she wants to go shopping with us?'

'Sure. And why don't you invite Carla and Lucy along, too?'

'Well, I hope you guys aren't planning on getting *my* present there,' David said. 'Because you won't find it. You'll have better luck finding it at a car dealer's – hint, hint.'

'No problem,' Chrissie said. 'In fact, we're buying you an entire lotful of cars. That way, you can just drive away in one of your fancy cars, and I'll have the horses all to myself.'

'Very funny, shrimp,' David responded with a sour look.

Ignoring him, Chrissie sprang up from the table. 'I'd better go call Debbie now,' she said.

She was halfway out the kitchen door when she heard her father's stern voice. 'Chrissie, finish your breakfast first. You've got to learn how to eat better. I can't have a scrawny little kid raising my horses.'

'But Dad,' Chrissie said, moaning, 'I won't be able to ride a horse if I'm a blimp.'

'No arguments, Chrissie. Finish your breakfast so we can get some work done at the barn before your shopping trip.' He looked at David. 'And you, too,' he said. 'Both of you should hurry up and get down there.' Then he turned abruptly and strode out of the kitchen.

Chrissie went back to her chair and wolfed down the rest of her food. When she was through eating, she got up and put her dishes in the sink.

'If the girls want to come with us, tell them to be here by ten,' Mrs. Williams called out as Chrissie ran upstairs.

11

Chrissie picked up her phone and pressed the automatic-dial button for Debbie's number. Then she rolled on to her bed.

'Calling all shoppers,' she said, giggling, when Debbie answered. 'Mobilise for an exciting store adventure.'

'Yes!' Debbie yelled. 'But this is a switch. Since when do the shops win out over the barn?'

'My mother's on a mission,' Chrissie explained. 'She's making me go. And if I have to go, so do you. Besides, I think I might have heard something about a sale . . .'

'I'll be right there,' Debbie said.

'Come over as soon as you can. I have to go now, because I want to check on Excellence before we leave, and I still have to call Lucy and Carla to see if they want to come.'

'I'll call them,' Debbie offered.

'Oh, thank you! You're the best friend anyone could have,' Chrissie said.

'I don't know, Chrissie,' Debbie said good-humouredly. 'I'd say that horse was your real best friend.'

Chrissie knew her friend was just kidding, but there was also a hint of truth in what she was saying. 'No way. Never!' she exclaimed. 'It's just that I'm so excited about my birthday. When I turn thirteen I'll—'

'—get a foal to care for, earn a salary, and

12

won't get treated like a kid anymore,' Debbie finished for her.

'Uh-oh, have I been *that* boring?' Chrissie asked.

'No,' answered Debbie. 'It's just that I've been your best friend since nursery and turning thirteen is pretty much all you've talked about for the last five years!'

'That bad, huh?'

'Almost!'

'I'm sorry. But it's all so exciting, and I want you to be a part of everything. Excellence is about to give birth and I want you to help me with her foal.'

'I have a much better idea,' Debbie said. 'You raise it and I'll watch from a distance.'

Chrissie laughed. 'I guess that's better than nothing. Well, I'll see you later – if you think you can stand to spend an entire day with me.'

'I'll just have to grin and bear it,' Debbie said, laughing. 'Bye!'

After hanging up, Chrissie raced out of the house and towards the foaling and yearling barn. She spotted her father at the corral, so she rushed over to him. He was leaning against a fence, watching the horses graze.

'Look around, honey,' Mr. Williams said, putting his hand on Chrissie's shoulder. 'This is what it's all about. All of the long hours and hard work we've put into the farm have really paid off.' He looked into Chrissie's eyes. 'Who knows? Someday this might all be yours.'

Chrissie smiled at her father. She loved coming out every morning to check on the horses with him. David and Mrs. Williams were quite happy living on the farm, but to Chrissie and her father, the farm and the horses meant everything in the world.

Chrissie looked out over the farm. The bright red barns and stables stood out in sharp contrast to the snow-covered pastures. She took a deep breath of crisp country air, and felt a surge of pride. The land was so beautiful. This was where she wanted to be. She exhaled and watched her breath billow out in great white clouds.

She and her father walked towards the foaling and yearling barn, which was the largest of the four barns on the farm. The mares and their newborns lived there, along with the yearlings that would soon be sold at the auction.

John Patterson, the manager of the farm, was waiting for them in the tack room at the east end of the barn.

'Hello, John,' said Mr. Williams. 'Anything going on?'

'Nope,' he said as he scratched his neck. 'There's nothing new to report this morning. All the mares seem to be doing well, and the yearlings look terrific. You know, I think the

14

winner of this year's yearling herd is going to be First Try.' He nodded his head thoughtfully. 'Yup. I'd stake my reputation on it.'

Chrissie walked over to First Try's stall and peered in. She was a beautiful ten-month-old filly and one of the farm's first Anglo-Arab crossbreeds. Dr. Anderson had convinced Chrissie's father to try crossbreeding some of his Thoroughbred mares with a neighbour's prize Arabian stallion, and her father had taken the vet's advice. If the experiment was a success, then the horses would turn out with the best features of each breed, and they would fetch a high price at the yearling auction.

'Gee, I'm surprised she's not bigger,' Chrissie said after studying the animal for a few minutes. 'She's at least two hands shorter than any of the Thoroughbred yearlings.'

'Well, that's not really surprising,' her father explained. 'Arabians are smaller than Thoroughbreds, so it makes sense that a part-Arabian foal is a little bit smaller than a Thoroughbred foal.' He came over next to Chrissie and looked into the stall. 'I happen to think she's a real beauty.'

Chrissie nodded. The foal was beautiful in its own odd way, but it would take some time to get used to the new breed. 'Well, the Thoroughbreds are a lot sleeker and more graceful. This one looks so . . . so awkward.'

Chrissie stared at the wide-eyed yearling a little bit longer, then turned to face her father. 'Anyway, I think I'll go check on Excellence now.'

'Go ahead,' her father said. 'But before you do, how about making sure all the horses have been fed? And please check that their water buckets are full, too. The grooms were busy with White Stockings this morning – she hasn't been acting right. So everybody here's running a little behind.'

'No problem, Dad,' Chrissie called over her shoulder as she ran down the barn aisle. She went over to the water hose and grabbed a bucket from the shelf above it. Then she filled it to the brim and headed over to the first stall. Six of the stalls in the foaling and yearling barn were occupied by horses to be sold at the upcoming yearling sale. The rest of the stalls held mares due to deliver foals sometime after the first of the year.

Chrissie needed both hands and all her strength to carry the water bucket, and even then she could only just manage. At four feet nine inches, she weighed only eighty-two pounds. She was shorter than all her friends, and she barely weighed more than the dog – a fact that her brother never let her forget. *Maybe this year I'll really grow*, she thought as she went to fill up another bucket.

16

By the time Chrissie finished watering the horses, her jeans were soaked.

'Isn't it a little cold for swimming?' David said from behind her.

'Ha, ha. You're so funny,' Chrissie said, turning to face him. 'Jingles got a little too playful and knocked over the bucket.'

David picked a long piece of straw out of Chrissie's wavy hair. 'Knocked you down, too, huh, shorty?' he said with a grin.

'Listen,' she said, putting her hands on her hips. 'It's not my fault I got all the brains and you got all the height!'

David laughed. 'Okay. You win, shorty. So, have you checked the food chart yet?'

The food chart listed what quantity and type of food each horse was supposed to get, and it also showed whether a horse was supposed to get any other supplements. One of Chrissie's jobs was to measure out the horses' supplemental feed and give it to them.

'I was just going to check the chart now,' Chrissie answered, tossing her long brown hair.

'I'll do it,' David offered. 'Mum's waiting for you, so why don't you go check on Excellence, then head on back to the house?'

'Thanks, David,' Chrissie said happily. She walked over to the carrot bin and pulled out a handful of carrots for Excellence.

When she got to the mare's stall, she leaned

over the lower half of the wooden door. 'Look what I've got for you, Excellence!' Chrissie called, holding out a carrot in the palm of her hand.

Excellence made her way over to Chrissie, moving as quickly as a pregnant mare could. She lipped up the carrot and chomped on it noisily.

'Can I come in?' Chrissie asked the horse. Then she smiled. 'Boy, if you ever answered me, would I be surprised!'

She opened the stall door and started to walk in, but when she saw Excellence lay back her ears, she immediately pulled away. Chrissie knew the mare's ears were signalling that she was nervous, which meant that Chrissie had to be extra careful. Even though Excellence knew Chrissie and liked her, she might have been feeling a little jittery because of her pregnancy.

Chrissie let Excellence take another carrot from her hand before walking back into the stall. 'How are you doing, girl?' she said in a gentle tone. 'Feeling okay?' Chrissie continued to talk as she let the horse sniff her hand. Then she went over to her side and began stroking her neck.

Once the mare relaxed a bit, Chrissie wrapped her arms around Excellence's neck and pressed her face against the horse's warm side. Excellence snorted with pleasure. Then Chrissie held the horse's head in her hands and planted

18

a big kiss on her nose. She thought she saw a glimmer of happiness and expectation in Excellence's glistening brown eyes.

'Your baby's going to be the most beautiful foal ever. I'm going to take really good care of it. Don't you worry. I'll be a great baby-horse sitter.'

Suddenly the intercom crackled. The farm had a simple communication system set up between the house and each of the barns. 'Chrissie, come on back to the house,' Mrs. Williams said through the static. 'Debbie's here.'

Chrissie gave Excellence a final pat on the neck and, after making sure the stall door was closed behind her, ran out of the barn and up to the house.

Two

CHRISSIE WAVED WHEN SHE SAW DEBBIE SITTING ON
the front steps, waiting for her.

'Hi!' Debbie called out as she stood up. 'Your
mum says she'll be right out. So, how's
Excellence doing?'

'Great!' Chrissie said cheerfully. 'Do you want
to see her when we get back?'

'Sure,' Debbie said. 'You might turn me on to
horses yet, though I think I'd have a hard time
getting my parents to buy me one. They won't
even let me get a cat.'

'I wish we could spend the whole day at the
barn, but Mum is really set on this shopping
trip,' Chrissie said glumly. 'And I still have to
get a couple of Christmas gifts.'

'Oh, cheer up. It'll be fun, Chrissie. And your
mum told me she was going to get you some

new clothes – jeans and stuff.'

Chrissie made a face, then popped her head in through the front door. 'Mum!' she called out. 'I thought we were only going *Christmas* shopping.'

'We are,' her mother answered, walking towards them. 'But I thought we'd also do some *Chrissie* shopping. You really need some new things.'

'Oh, all right,' Chrissie said reluctantly. 'Let's get this over with.'

Debbie chuckled and shook her head at Chrissie's impatience.

'Are Carla and Lucy coming, too?' Chrissie's mother asked.

'No,' Debbie answered. 'I called them up, but they're busy painting Lucy's bedroom.'

'Okay, then,' Mrs. Williams said. 'Let's hit the road.' She pulled on her ski jacket and grabbed her purse and keys. Chrissie and Debbie followed Mrs. Williams over to the jeep.

'How are the mares doing?' Debbie asked as Mrs. Williams turned a corner.

'Oh, they're just fine,' Mrs. Williams responded.

'Especially Excellence. She's in perfect condition!' Chrissie said, beaming. 'Her foal is going to be amazing.' She looked at her mother. 'We'd better hurry up, Mum,' she said. 'I want to take Debbie to the barn later.'

'Don't worry, Chrissie. I promise we'll be back before the foal is born,' her mother teased.

When they got to the department store, Chrissie and Debbie went off on their own to do their Christmas shopping, and Mrs. Williams agreed to meet them in the juniors' department in one hour.

'Do you still have a lot of gifts to get?' Debbie asked as they made their way through the mall.

'Actually, I need only two more – David's and Mum's,' Chrissie answered.

'Really? You have everyone else's gifts? Does that mean you've already got mine?' Debbie asked excitedly.

'Of course. You're easy to shop for, you big clothes-horse.' Chrissie knew clothing was what Debbie wanted for Christmas. Besides a cat, that is.

'So,' Debbie said nonchalantly, 'how about if I tell you what I got you, and you tell me what you got me?'

Chrissie laughed. 'You couldn't get me to tell you if you tortured me. You'll just have to be patient like everyone else and wait till Christmas.'

'Oh, come on, Chrissie,' Debbie urged. 'Please.'

'Well . . . maybe I'll tell you what colour it is if you help me find presents for David and Mum.'

'You've got a deal,' Debbie said quickly 'I know. Let's head over to the bookshop first. David could probably use some sort of college survival guide, and your mother might enjoy a good romance.'

'That's a great idea,' Chrissie said, turning around and heading towards the bookshop. 'And by the way, you're going to look fabulous in lavender.'

By the time the girls met up with Mrs. Williams, Chrissie was itching to go back to the farm. But her mother had other ideas.

'Sorry, Chrissie,' her mother told her. 'You need some jeans and at least two new shirts. And we should also get you a nice outfit to wear on Christmas Day. After that, we can go.'

Chrissie chose a pair of jeans to wear around the barn and another pair for school. Then she and her mother tried to find a skirt and blouse they both liked. When they finally agreed on something, her mother asked her to try on a couple of heavy flannel shirts for working around the farm. Finally, after all that, they were done.

'Come on, let's get out of here!' Chrissie said impatiently as soon as the clothes were paid for.

Her mother shook her head, smiling. 'How did I end up with a daughter who has absolutely no interest in clothes?' she said to Debbie.

23

'Maybe Debbie and I were swapped at birth,' Chrissie quipped. 'She *loves* to go shopping – even more than you do, Mum.'

Chrissie's mother laughed. 'You'll change your mind about clothes when you get older,' she said as she ruffled Chrissie's hair.

'Don't count on it,' Chrissie said, making a face. 'Come on, you guys. Excellence is waiting.'

When they got back to the farm, Chrissie led Debbie directly to the foaling and yearling barn. The pregnant mare gave them a big snort of welcome as they approached her stall.

'Wow! You weren't kidding. She *is* big!' Debbie exclaimed. 'I can't believe how much her belly has grown in two weeks.'

'I know. I can't wait to see the baby,' Chrissie said as she offered Excellence a carrot.

'*You* can't wait? How do you think the mother feels?' a voice said from behind them.

Chrissie turned around. 'Dr. Anderson!' she said in surprise as she went over to meet her. 'Hi! I thought you were coming earlier. But I'm glad I didn't miss your visit.'

'I had to take care of an emergency over at the Baker farm before coming here,' Dr. Anderson explained. Then she looked over at Debbie. 'Hi, Debbie,' she said warmly. 'It's nice to see you, too.'

'Hi, Dr. Anderson,' Debbie said, smiling.

Dr. Judith Anderson had set up her practice

24

in Middletown shortly before Chrissie was born. Because Chrissie thought she might want to become a vet one day, she often tagged along with the doctor when she made her rounds on the farm. Dr. Anderson knew how much Chrissie loved the horses, and she never got tired of answering her questions.

'So when's it going to happen? When do you think Excellence will foal?' Chrissie asked.

'Well, I'll examine her right now and let you know.'

Dr. Anderson went into the mare's stall and took out her stethoscope. But before beginning the examination, she stroked Excellence's neck and talked to her softly.

As the girls watched the doctor work, Chrissie's father and Mr. Patterson came over and joined them. Dr. Anderson took Excellence's temperature and then checked her pulse.

'Thirty-two beats per minute,' she announced with a smile. 'Perfect!'

'Everything look okay?' Chrissie's father asked.

'You bet. But she does seem a little further along than we thought. She looks just about ready to foal, you know.'

Mr. Williams nodded. 'We'll keep an eye on her.'

The adults moved on to the next stall, but Chrissie and Debbie stayed behind with Excellence.

25

'Ohhhh!' Chrissie said as soon as they left. 'I can't wait. I really want to raise Excellence's foal!'

'Well, you don't have that much longer to wait. And we have only a week of school left before the Christmas holiday starts. After that you can totally desert me and start spending all your time with Excellence,' Debbie said. She looked up at the big clock on the wall. 'Uh-oh! I have to get back to the house. My mum is going to be here any minute to pick me up.'

'I'll walk you back,' Chrissie said.

Debbie's mum was just pulling up when they got to the house. 'Bye, Chrissie!' Debbie said, jumping into the car. 'Thanks for taking me shopping.'

Chrissie waved as the car pulled away and drove out of sight. Then she ran back to the foaling and yearling barn. Since she'd finished her chores earlier, Chrissie had some time to go out on her favourite riding horse, Tuskers. She went into the tack room, grabbed a saddle off a rack, and lugged it over to Tuskers's stall. Though he was a gelding, he was stabled together with the mares because he seemed to have a calming effect on them. The Williamses kept four other horses exclusively for riding, but Tuskers was the one Chrissie rode all the time. He was eighteen years old and very gentle.

'Hi, Tuskers,' Chrissie said as she hung his saddle on a nearby rack. 'Do you want to go for a ride?' She held out a hand and let him sniff it, then she led him out of his stall and into the aisle. She hooked him up to the cross-ties, talking to him as they went along. Then she began to groom him lightly, starting at his head and neck and working backwards, towards his tail. When his body was dust-free, she brushed each of his legs and used the hoof pick to clean out the dirt in his hoofs.

'There,' Chrissie said, standing back to look at him. 'You look great. Now we have to get a saddle on you, don't we?' She dragged over a step-stool and, with the saddle cradled in her arms, got on top of it. It was a bit tricky to keep her balance while carrying the saddle, but there was no other way she could reach up high enough to get the saddle on Tuskers's back.

'I wish I would just *grow,* already,' Chrissie muttered as she positioned the saddle over Tuskers's withers.

Saddle in place, she stepped down off the stool to fasten the girth around his belly. When she had got it as tight as she could, she took his bridle off the hook on the wall and walked over to him. As soon as she unhooked the cross-ties from his halter, Tuskers lowered his head so that Chrissie could take off his halter and put on the bridle.

'Good boy, Tuskers,' Chrissie said, praising him. 'You make it so easy to saddle you up.'

She removed the halter and slipped his bridle into place. After checking all the buckles one last time, Chrissie led him out of the barn.

She lowered the stirrup on the left-hand side of the saddle so that she could slide her foot into it and mount the horse. She swung up into the saddle and adjusted both stirrups to the right length.

'Are you ready, Tuskers?' she said, leaning forward, closer to his ears. 'Come on. Let's go.' She gave the left rein a gentle tug and squeezed with her thighs. Tuskers responded immediately and headed down the path towards the riding arena, which was mostly used by riders who boarded horses at Williams Farm.

'It's you and me, Tuskers,' Chrissie said as they entered the empty arena. 'We're going to be great at the summer shows!'

They began by warming up at a walk. Though he was one of their older horses, he still had a lot of spunk, and Chrissie loved him. Still, she felt ready for a younger show horse – one that could actually make it over a jump. There were a couple of younger riding horses at the farm, but only one of them was a good jumper, and Chrissie wasn't allowed to ride him because he spooked very easily. So the only way she was going to get a good jumping horse was if she waited until she could buy one herself with the money she earned from the sale of her yearling.

As Chrissie worked Tuskers, first at a walk, then at a trot, she looked longingly at the jumps set up in the middle of the arena. It was so frustrating that she couldn't do any jumping, and she imagined Tuskers might want to go over the jumps, too. But soon she had Tuskers cantering, and she didn't feel quite so frustrated any more. She rode him hard, pushing him to keep up a fast pace. With the wind blowing in her hair and Tuskers moving so gracefully beneath her, Chrissie felt as if she were on top of the world. Nothing beat riding in rhythm with the pounding of a horse's hoofs. It felt like flying.

When their workout was done, Chrissie slowed Tuskers down to a walk and gave him a lot of rein so that he could relax and cool down. She patted him on the neck as they circled the arena. 'Good boy, Tuskers. That was a great ride.' After a few minutes, the horse's breathing began to slow down, and Chrissie walked him up the path towards the barn.

'You're going to do so well at the hunter shows, but I wish I could jump with you,' Chrissie said sadly. She rode in silence for a few minutes, letting Tuskers take them back to the barn. He had been on the farm for so long that he knew his way around and didn't need to be guided. 'You know,' she said finally, 'I'm going to get a real show horse with the money I make at the auction – one that I can enter show jumping events with. But don't worry, Tuskers,' she added. 'I'll always love you!'

Three

WHEN THE FINAL BELL OF THE AUTUMN TERM RANG, Chrissie and Debbie tore down the school steps into the courtyard.

'Yes! Two weeks of Christmas holiday!' Debbie yelled happily. 'Two weeks of going shopping, seeing movies, and sleeping till noon!'

'It's going to be great!' Chrissie sang out. 'No homework. And I can hang out in the barn and ride Tuskers all I want.' She looked at her friend for a moment, then offered, 'I'll even go to two movies and spend an afternoon shopping with you.'

'Okay. And I'll spend two afternoons at the barn and help you clean tack for the auction.'

'Deal!' Chrissie said, shaking Debbie's hand.

That night at dinner, Mr. Williams outlined

what Chrissie and David had to do in preparation for the auction.

'David, I want you to make sure all the weanlings we're showing at the auction are ready. This means you have to do an extra careful job grooming and exercising them before next Friday.'

Mr. Williams took a sip of coffee before turning to Chrissie. 'And you, Chrissie . . . I want you to make sure all their tack is soaped, cleaned, and ready. Okay? And do a very thorough job cleaning out the stalls this week.'

Chrissie's heart sank, but she tried to hide her disappointment. She knew that the week before the auction was always hectic and that all jobs were important. The weanlings – foals less than a year old that no longer nursed from their mothers – would be groomed for showing, and their tack had to be inspected, polished, and repaired if necessary. Still, she wanted so badly to work with the horses.

She nodded silently.

'I also want you to check in on Excellence every couple of hours and report back to me if her condition changes. Okay?' her father added.

Chrissie's spirits immediately lifted, and she saw David wink at her from across the table. 'You can count on me, Dad,' she said brightly.

In the week that followed, all the grooms worked extra hard to help prepare for the auction. Everyone scurried around the barn areas frantically, making sure the yearlings would be ready on Friday.

By Thursday afternoon, Chrissie was exhausted. She was cleaning out one of the stalls when she decided to sit down for a while and take a break. After a minute or two, David came looking for her.

'I'm in here!' Chrissie yelled when she heard him calling her name.

'Hey, squirt, what's up?' he said, peering into the stall.

Chrissie looked up at him. 'Not much. But you know, I think I'm going to miss them.'

'Who?' David asked with a puzzled look on his face.

'The yearlings. They're like part of our family now. It feels strange to think about selling them.'

David sat down next to her on a pile of straw. 'I know. But get used to it. Next year you'll be selling your own horse.'

Chrissie nodded. 'I know. And I haven't forgotten rule number one – don't get attached.'

'It sounds like a snap,' he said, 'but believe me, it's not as easy as you'd think.'

Chrissie appreciated her brother's advice, but she didn't think she'd have a problem with getting too attached to the foal she raised. She was determined to take over the farm one day, and she was prepared to manage it professionally. If that meant not letting her emotions get in the way, then she wouldn't. Besides, the yearling she sold at the end of the next year would earn her enough money to buy a real show horse, and that was something she had wanted for a very long time.

That night was busier than any other night that week, but Chrissie had to find a way to talk to her parents. She wanted to ask them if she could skip the following day's auction and stay behind to keep an eye on the other horses – especially Excellence. She was excited about seeing the annual sale, but she felt it was more important to be with the pregnant mare.

She finally managed to pin them down when they went up to the house to get a quick bite to eat. 'Don't you think I should be here just in case she needs me?' Chrissie asked her parents hopefully.

'Mr. Patterson will be here to watch Excellence, so there really isn't any reason for you to stay home, too,' her father said. 'Besides,' he went on, 'next year you'll be showing your own yearling. You might want to take some notes.'

'You're right,' Chrissie agreed. 'It'll be good experience. Well, I guess I'll just go and check on her now.'

'All right, dear,' her mother said. 'But make

sure all your chores are done before you go to bed.'

Chrissie hurried down to the foaling and yearling barn. After she had given fresh water to all the horses and checked their blankets and leg wraps, she went into Excellence's stall.

She offered the beautiful horse a carrot, then began stroking her head and neck. 'You'll be fine, girl. Don't worry. I'm only going to be gone for the day. And as soon as we return tomorrow night, I'll come see you. Just make sure you don't have your baby while I'm gone. I really want to be here to help you out, okay?'

Excellence whinnied and bobbed her head up and down as though she understood Chrissie. Chrissie laughed and kissed the horse's soft muzzle before leaving the stall.

The farm was still bustling with activity hours after darkness fell. Getting the horses ready for the auction had everyone working much later than usual. Chrissie found Dr. Anderson and gave her a hand making sure that all of the horses had their forms and health certificates. These forms had to be handed over to the new owners when a horse was sold, because they contained important information about who the horse's parents were and what shots and vaccines the animal had received.

Mr. Patterson and the grooms were busy preparing the large horse vans for the trip. The insides of the vans had to be disinfected and made ready for the horses. All of the cross-ties that were used to keep the horses separated were checked and rechecked, the van floors had been covered in fresh bedding, the hay nets were inspected and filled, and the water buckets were filled and hung.

David was busy, too. He had to make sure the Williamses' jeep was loaded with first-aid kits, extra tack, rope, a fire extinguisher, the horses' various documents, and the Williams Farm banner.

After Chrissie finished cleaning and inspecting the tack, she helped the hands put down fresh hay in the vans. Finally, after a long, hard day, she dragged herself upstairs and stepped out of her work clothes without bothering to put them in the hamper. Hearing the sounds of the final preparations in the background, she drifted off to sleep and dreamed about showing Excellence's foal the following year.

The next morning, after breakfast, Chrissie went out to the barn to see if there was anything she could do to help out. The grooms were leading the yearlings out of their stalls and loading them into the vans, so she went to her father to offer her help.

'Uh, Dad,' she said, struggling to keep up

with him as he walked back and forth giving the grooms instructions, 'do you want me to help load the yearlings?'

Her father turned around and saw her at his heels. 'No, Chrissie. I think we have everything under control.'

'I could bring them out of their stalls.'

'Chrissie, the horses are nervous and it's just too dangerous for you,' he said firmly. 'If you want to help, then you can move the extra halters in the tack room to the jeep, okay?'

Chrissie held her tongue, but she really wanted to tell her father that he didn't give her enough credit. She knew she could handle the horses as well as any of the grooms, but her parents treated her like a child. She went into the tack room and strung both arms through as many halters as she could carry. Then she headed for the jeep, which was parked next to the horse vans.

'Here comes Thunder!' David called out as Mr. Patterson led the colt toward one of the vans.

Chrissie immediately approached the loading area to catch a glimpse of Excellence's last foal. *Is that what her new foal will look like when it's born?* she wondered. Then, as she was watching Thunder, she accidentally stepped on a rope attached to one of the halters and tripped. Halters scattered everywhere when she crashed to the ground.

Thunder spooked at the sudden movement and reared away from the van, pulling Mr. Patterson off balance. He fell on to the ramp with a loud thud.

Mr. Williams quickly leaped on to the ramp and grabbed Thunder's lead line before the horse could get loose. 'Whoa, boy,' he said as he tried to calm the horse. 'Whoa! That's it. Take it easy, boy. Easy! That's it, Thunder.'

As soon as Thunder had calmed down enough, Mr. Williams handed him back to Mr. Patterson and stalked over to Chrissie, who was trying to pick up all the halters.

'Chrissie! What are you doing?' Mr. Williams said angrily. 'You could have caused a real problem. Please go back to the house right now. You're just getting in the way out here!'

'But—'

'*Now*, Chrissie,' he said tightly. 'Just leave those halters here.'

Chrissie felt herself turning red from embarrassment. 'I was just trying to help,' she said softly, trying to hold back her tears. She turned and ran to the house.

David ran after her and found her in the kitchen, sobbing. He came over and put an arm around her shaking shoulders.

'I was just trying to help,' Chrissie choked out. 'I tripped. That's all.'

38

'Hey, don't worry. Dad knows that. He'll apologise when he cools off.'

'Everybody treats me like a little baby around here. I'm almost thirteen. It's not my fault the halters drag on the ground when I carry them. I'm short. Is that my fault?'

'No, of course it isn't,' he said in a comforting tone. 'And you're not short, Chrissie. Your feet reach all the way to the ground, don't they?'

Chrissie looked up and gave her brother a half smile. Then she felt herself growing angry at her parents, especially her father. 'Okay, fine! I'll stay out of their way, but if they want my help, they're going to have to come and find me. I'm not coming out of my room until we're ready to go. In fact, I may not come out even if they ask me!' she said indignantly.

David grinned. 'That's the spirit. The mouse that roared is back in top form. Well, I'd better get back out there and help.'

As David had predicted, her father *did* come upstairs and apologise to Chrissie before they left for the auction. Chrissie had calmed down by then, so she made up with him right away.

The trip to the auction was uneventful, and as soon as they got there they began setting up the stalls and unloading the horses. When they were almost finished with the preparations, Chrissie decided to take a walk and look around.

'Just make sure you're back by two,' her mother told her. 'That's when we have to start getting our horses ready.'

'I will, Mum,' Chrissie replied.

She spent the next couple of hours looking at the yearlings other farms were going to be auctioning off, and she wasn't particularly impressed with what she saw. The Williamses' Thoroughbreds really seemed to be among the best.

By the time she returned to their holding corral the yearlings were already being led out to the main corral. And by three forty-five, all the horses had been sold. Chrissie couldn't believe it! It had taken them a whole year to raise those horses, and now they belonged to other owners.

Later that evening the Williamses sat down to a special celebration dinner at home. The sale had gone even better than expected, and the Williams Farm yearlings had fetched top price at the auction.

'Boy, could you believe the bidding war for Thunder?' Chrissie said with a mouth full of salad. 'I didn't think anyone would pay ten thousand dollars for a horse.'

'Well, if everything works out, Excellence's new foal should bring in even more money next year,' Mr. Williams said.

'I hope so,' Chrissie said softly. *I could buy the*

40

jumper of my dreams with all that money, she thought.

She imagined running across a field of wildflowers with a sleek, well-muscled colt or filly at her side. Maybe she'd call the new foal Wildflower . . . She smiled softly at her fantasy.

David punched her in the arm. 'What's the joke, shrimp?'

'Nothing,' she said, blushing as her parents gave her puzzled looks. But she knew the foal would be something – something important and precious to her. Maybe she'd name the foal Precious. Or Chestnut Beauty. Or even Chrissie's Dream . . .

Four

ON THE DAY BEFORE CHRISTMAS, CHRISSIE WENT DOWN
to the foaling and yearling barn right after
breakfast, just as she'd done every day of her
holiday, and arrived in time to watch Dr.
Anderson examine Excellence. She stood
quietly outside the stall as the vet felt the mare's
teats.

'I'm doing this to figure out how soon she'll
foal,' Dr. Anderson explained, looking up at
Chrissie. After a few seconds, the vet frowned
and shook her head. Chrissie felt her stomach
tighten.

'W-what's wrong?' Chrissie asked.

'Shhh.' Dr. Anderson held up a hand to silence
Chrissie. 'Give me a minute.'

The doctor gently squeezed the mare's teats.
Milk appeared. Chrissie drew a sharp breath.

She knew what that meant. The foal would probably be born that day!

Then the vet took Excellence's temperature, and Chrissie bit her lip in an effort to keep silent. She was aching to know what was going on.

When she finished the examination, Dr. Anderson rushed by Chrissie and headed up to the house. Alarmed, Chrissie followed close behind her.

Mr. and Mrs. Williams, Mr. Patterson, and David were sitting at the kitchen table talking about the horses that had been sold at the auction.

'We've got a problem,' Dr. Anderson announced as she strode in. 'I think you'd all better get ready to spend some time at the barn this afternoon.'

'Excellence?' Mr. Williams said, rising quickly to his feet.

The vet nodded. 'She'll be delivering sometime within the next twenty-four hours.'

'Oh, dear,' Mrs. Williams said, shaking her head.

Chrissie looked at her mother's worried expression and felt her stomach tighten even more. If Excellence delivered before January first, her foal couldn't be sold as a yearling the following year.

Because all Thoroughbreds are given a birthday of January first, even if they're born in

43

March or April, horse breeders try to breed their mares so that the foals are born just after the New Year. That way, by the time the horses are sold at the December auctions, the foals are just under twelve months old and they look older and more mature. Less-developed foals didn't fetch very high prices at the auction.

'It just doesn't seem fair,' Chrissie said softly. She slumped down into a chair, feeling disappointment well up inside her. Even though Excellence's foal would be only a little more than a year old, it would still be considered a two-year-old at the next auction and would not bring as much money. And Excellence's foals were so important to the farm. If it was born prematurely, it might require a lot more care and expensive veterinary treatment during its first couple of months.

' . . . so I'll assign one of the grooms to keep a night watch on Excellence,' Mr. Patterson was saying. 'Just as a precaution.'

'If you need me, I'll be happy to take a shift, too,' David volunteered.

'Thanks. That would be great,' Mr. Patterson replied. 'I can use all the help I can get.'

'I can help, too!' Chrissie blurted out. 'At least for tonight. It's not a school night . . . and I could even spend the night at the barn.' She gave each of her parents a pleading look.

'Please, Mum? Dad?'

Mrs. Williams shrugged. 'Well, since you're still on vacation, it's fine with me. Bob?'

'Oh, can I, Dad?' Chrissie said, getting up from her chair.

'If you finish all your chores and take a nap this afternoon, you can spend the night in the barn,' he answered, smiling.

'You got it,' Chrissie said with a huge grin. 'And I'll even finish the maths assignment we're supposed to do over the holiday.'

That night after dinner, David helped Chrissie set up a cot right outside Excellence's stall.

'Are you going to be all right?' he asked. 'Warm enough?'

Chrissie nodded. 'Yeah. And I even brought a thermos of hot cocoa, a radio, and a book so that I won't fall asleep.'

David smiled. 'Aren't you the professional!' he teased. 'Well, if you need anything, just buzz me over the intercom. Okay?'

'Okay.'

'See you in the morning,' he said as he headed out of the barn.

'Good night, David . . . and thanks,' Chrissie called out after him.

Chrissie shifted around on the cot until she found a comfortable position. She loved being there alone with the horses, breathing in air that smelled of hay.

Soon the horses stopped moving around in

their stalls, and Chrissie knew they were settling in for the night.

When it was almost one o'clock in the morning, and Chrissie was beginning to doze off, she heard Excellence snorting and moving around in her stall. Chrissie leaped out of the cot instantly and looked into the stall. Excellence's nostrils were flaring and she was trying to lie down. *This is it*, Chrissie thought. *She's going to give birth.*

Chrissie ran over to the intercom and switched it on. 'Mum! Dad! Get up! I think Excellence is going into labour!'

'I'll be right there!' her father answered over the speaker.

In about a minute he ran into the barn, wearing boots and a parka over his pyjamas.

'Good work!' he said to Chrissie as he went over to Excellence's stall. He examined the mare. 'You were right to call me, sweetie. She's definitely going into labour. Your mother's calling the vet right now.'

Chrissie glowed with pleasure at the praise.

'Come here and give me a hand with her,' her father said with an encouraging smile.

Quickly they wrapped Excellence's tail. Then Mr. Williams got a towel, soaked it in antiseptic, and wiped the mare's hindquarters clean. The vet got to the stall a few minutes after they had finished the preparations for the mare's labour.

'Okay, everybody out!' Dr. Anderson shooed them out of the stall. 'Let's see if she can do this herself.'

For the next hour, the three of them watched as the foal was being born. Chrissie held her breath practically the entire time. Although Chrissie had seen many foals delivered before, the sight of a foal coming out of its mother never ceased to amaze her. With Excellence lying on her side, the foal's forelegs slipped out, followed by its nose. Then, slowly, its body and hind legs appeared.

At two twenty-two on Christmas Day, just an hour and a half after she began labour, Excellence was the proud mother of a baby boy. Although the colt was a couple of weeks early, he appeared to be healthy and was soon standing up by himself.

Chrissie gasped in awe of the little horse. He was beautiful! He had dark, wet fur with a small white patch on his face and four white stockings on his legs. Somehow he managed to remain standing, although it looked as if he might fall down at any second.

Dr. Anderson helped him find his mother's nipple and, while he nursed, she checked to make sure mother and baby were in good health. After a minute, the doctor looked up and gave Chrissie and her father a thumbs up.

Chrissie could see the relief on her father's

face. Premature foals often had dangerous medical problems, but this time the Williamses were lucky. The delivery had been easy, and the foal looked strong.

'You've got yourself quite a beauty,' Dr. Anderson said as she took off the rubber birthing sleeves and gloves she had put on before handling the new foal.

Mr. Williams was smiling like a proud father, but Chrissie knew he had to be disappointed that the foal had been born before the first of the year. As a two-year-old, the colt would be at a real disadvantage next December.

'Well, what should we call him?' Mr. Williams asked, looking around him. 'Any suggestions?'

'How about Outstanding?' Chrissie suggested enthusiastically. 'I think he's the most outstanding colt I've ever seen!'

Mr. Williams laughed. 'All right, Chrissie. If he's the most outstanding colt you've ever seen, then Outstanding's his name!'

'You've named him well,' Dr. Anderson said, laughing also.

'But now,' Chrissie's father added, 'you have to go up to the house and go to bed. It's past two o'clock in the morning. We'll open our presents when you get up later. Okay?'

Chrissie wanted to stay in the barn the rest of the night to be with Excellence and Outstanding, but she knew it was a bad idea to argue with her father when he was tired. Besides, a bed sounded great after all the hours she'd spent staying awake on the uncomfortable cot.

'Fine,' she called out over her shoulder as she left the barn, 'but I won't be able to sleep one bit!'

Chrissie crawled into bed, thinking about the next day. She couldn't wait to spend the entire day watching Outstanding bond with his mother – and with her!

My very own foal, she thought dreamily as she fell asleep. *The best Christmas present ever . . .*

Five

FOR THE NEXT WEEK, CHRISSIE SPENT EVERY FREE moment she had with Excellence and her baby. She'd seen hundreds of foals before, but none could compare to Outstanding. Even though he'd been born prematurely, he was strong-limbed and very athletic, with a gleaming coat. Everyone on the farm agreed – he was going to be one exceptional colt.

Debbie came over the day after Christmas and Chrissie took her to the barn to see Outstanding.

'Hey, Chrissie,' Debbie finally said, 'you weren't kidding. He's—'

'Amazing,' Chrissie said, finishing the sentence for her.

Debbie laughed. 'I think Outstanding pretty much says it all. And you're acting like a proud mother,' she teased. 'But don't you think this foal deserves some time alone with his real mother? Why don't we go riding or something?'

'Oh, that's a great idea!' Chrissie said. 'Come on. I'll saddle Tuskers and Blue Moon.'

About half an hour later, Chrissie and Debbie were mounted and circling the arena.

'I think I might take a couple of extra days holiday before going back to school,' Chrissie told her friend. 'I want to spend more time with Outstanding.'

'Chrissie, I know you really like that horse, but your parents are never going to go for that idea,' Debbie pointed out. 'You *have* to go to school. It's the law.'

'Well, maybe I can convince them that Outstanding really needs me. He was born prematurely, you know. And I think I can help him pull through.'

'Outstanding is doing just fine on his own,' Debbie said, sounding a little exasperated. 'You're not being realistic, Chrissie. Next thing you know, you'll be quitting the Save the Animals club so you can spend more time with that colt. And you're the president.'

Chrissie frowned. 'Actually, now that you mention it, that's exactly what I should do.'

'Hey, you can't do that! As vice-president, I would have to take over. That's not fair!'

'I'm sorry, but you've got to try to understand.

51

This is a special situation.'

Debbie sighed. 'Well, do what you like, but I still don't think your folks are going to let you miss school.'

Chrissie knew her friend was probably right, but she decided she would ask them anyway – when the time was right.

The night before school started up again, Chrissie told her parents about her plan to stay home for a few more days to care for the colt. 'After all,' she argued, 'nothing important ever happens in school for the first couple of days after Christmas. And I could also help out around the farm . . . I'd do an *outstanding* job.' She smiled at her own joke. 'What do you think?'

'No way, kiddo. You have to go to school!' her father said. 'Besides, you'll soon have plenty of opportunity to look after a foal.'

The next morning, Chrissie stopped by to say hello to Outstanding before she walked out to the front gates to wait for the school bus.

'Hey, Chrissie, I saved you a seat!' Debbie shouted from the window as the bus pulled up.

Chrissie got on the bus and plopped down next to Debbie. Carla and Lucy sat directly across the aisle.

'I can't believe our holiday ended so soon,' Debbie said with a groan. Chrissie was glad Debbie didn't embarrass her by saying something in front of Carla and Lucy about her failed plan to miss school. 'Now we have nothing to look forward to until Easter.'

'Just months of boring school,' Carla put in.

'Don't remind me,' Lucy said as she rummaged through her lunch bag to see what was in it.

'Oh, yes we do!' Chrissie announced happily. 'My mother's taking us into New York City for my birthday.'

'No kidding? Where are we going? Bloomingdale's? Saks?' Debbie asked.

'I don't think so,' Chrissie said with an amused grin on her face. 'It's *my* birthday, after all. Besides, my mother won't tell me. It's going to be a surprise.'

'Well,' Debbie said thoughtfully, 'even if we don't do any shopping, it sounds pretty good to me. But we still have a whole month to go before your birthday – a long month with lots and lots of homework.'

Chrissie nodded. *At least I have Outstanding to keep me happy*, she thought.

As the bus pulled up in front of the school Debbie jumped up from her seat. 'Look!' she said. 'There's Billy Davis. Isn't he cute?'

'He's awesome,' Carla answered.

Chrissie looked at the boy Debbie was pointing to and shrugged. 'I guess so,' she said without much enthusiasm. Then she rolled her eyes when she realised Debbie was checking her hair in a small mirror.

As they were getting off the bus Debbie turned to Chrissie. 'You'll come around,' she said with a knowing smile. 'Boys are far more interesting than horses. You just have to give them a chance.'

'I'll *never* "come around",' Chrissie said, smiling at her friends. 'Outstanding is the only boy for me.' She batted her eyelashes and made kissing noises with her lips, and they all laughed.

During the next couple of weeks, Chrissie's teachers all made valiant efforts to fill her head with historical names and dates, Spanish verb conjugations, and the reasons why plants produce oxygen. But all she could think about was Outstanding. Every day she would rush home after school to change into her work clothes and run out to the barn.

On some afternoons, she would ride Tuskers first and then play with Outstanding and visit Excellence. Sometimes, when there was a newly born foal, she would go and check it out. There was always so much to do at the barn.

Then, one afternoon in late January, Chrissie arrived home and couldn't find anyone.

'Mum? Dad? Hey, where is everybody?' she shouted as she checked every room in the house.

Then she decided to see if they were all down at the barn. She was almost there when she saw Dr. Anderson, who was just leaving.

'Chrissie, go and see the new foal,' the doctor said. 'He's a real beauty.'

Chrissie ran into the barn and found her parents standing in the aisle outside of a stall.

'Chrissie,' her father said when he saw her, 'come and meet Squire's Boy.'

Chrissie peered over the stall door in the dim light of the barn. Inside was a chestnut foal struggling to stand up. Over and over again, his spindly legs tried to push his body off the ground, but each time, he folded over into a heap. Chrissie stared at the little horse for a minute, then turned to her father. 'Aren't his legs too long for his body?' she asked.

'No. Remember, he's not a Thoroughbred. He's an Anglo-Arab.'

'Oh. No wonder he doesn't look anything like Outstanding. But I guess he's kind of cute,' she added doubtfully.

Chrissie's father laughed. 'Kind of cute? He's perfect. I really think these Anglo-Arabs are going to be a big moneymaker for the farm.'

'Sure, Dad,' Chrissie said, wondering how her father could possibly think the foal was perfect. Outstanding was perfect – graceful and beautifully shaped. This foal had strange proportions, and it didn't even seem very strong or coordinated. 'Well, I'd better go do my chores now,' she said. She didn't mean to be rude to her father, but she wanted to get all her chores done so she could spend some time with Outstanding before dinner.

Chrissie did all her tasks as quickly as she could. She made sure all the water buckets were full, and then she checked on the mares and their new foals. Then, after giving the horses their supplemental feedings, she headed over to Excellence's stall.

'Hi, Excellence. Hi, Outstanding.' The little colt knew Chrissie by now and came trotting over to the stall door to receive his daily dose of affection.

Chrissie grabbed a currycomb from a basket and swung open the stall door. She stepped inside and went over to let Excellence sniff her. Then Chrissie began currying Outstanding by moving the comb through his coat in slow, even circles. Soon the colt's chestnut coat shone brightly.

'You'll be mine soon,' Chrissie whispered into Outstanding's ear as she brushed his head. 'My birthday's on February tenth, and that's coming up real fast. My sign's Aquarius, and I think you're Capricorn, but I think we're a perfect match anyway, don't you? Hey, can you keep a secret, boy?' Chrissie said as she ran the comb through his forelock. 'I think you're going to make the perfect birthday present.'

Even though it was a Saturday, Chrissie awoke on the morning of her birthday well before the alarm went off. 'Yes!' she shouted at the top of her lungs, jumping out of bed. 'I'm finally a teenager!'

Chrissie heard a banging sound coming through her wall and knew it was David, whose room was right next to hers. 'Hey, it's six o'clock in the morning! Keep it down in there!' he yelled through the wall.

'Sorry!' Chrissie shouted back unapologetically. It was finally her thirteenth birthday, and she felt like queen of the house. *David had better realise that things are going to change around here*, she thought. *I'm a teenager now and I deserve some respect.* She smiled at her feelings of self-importance, then put on her robe and headed to the bathroom.

After breakfast she hurried through her chores. She had to be done by midmorning because she was expecting Debbie, Carla, and Lucy to arrive at eleven. Chrissie still had no idea what her mother had planned for them to do in the city, but she knew it was going to be something special.

By ten forty-five, the three girls had arrived at the Williamses', bearing Chrissie's birthday presents.

'We'll open them later with all the others,' Mrs. Williams told the girls, much to Chrissie's dismay. 'For now, why don't you put them in the family room? We have to be on our way now, ladies. We don't want to get home too late tonight.'

It took almost an hour for them to get into Manhattan, and the whole way over, Chrissie kept pressing her mother to reveal details about the day's activities.

'Okay! Okay!' Mrs. Williams said finally. 'We're going to see a show at Radio City Music Hall, then I thought I'd take you to have a bite to eat at Rumplemayer's, and then we'll go back home to open presents and have your usual birthday dinner.'

Chrissie cheered. Her parents had taken her to Radio City once before, when she was six, and she'd loved the live show and the huge theatre. She had always wanted to go back there again, but she hadn't had another opportunity.

An hour later, as the lights in the theatre dimmed, Chrissie squirmed in her seat. This was going to be the greatest birthday ever. And the best part was still to come. For the next two hours, she lost herself in the magic of the show, temporarily transported by the music and the dancing.

It was almost three thirty when the doors to the music hall opened and the five theatregoers walked out into the fading afternoon sunlight of New York City.

'I'm starving!' Chrissie said as she looked around the busy street.

'Well, come on, then. Let's take a walk to Rumplemayer's,' her mother said, heading up the Avenue of the Americas. Chrissie, Debbie, Carla, and Lucy followed.

'I love New York,' Debbie said as they wove their way through the crowds. 'There's so much excitement – and great shops, too.'

'Yeah, I guess,' Chrissie conceded. 'But I don't think I'd want to live here.'

'Let me guess,' Carla interrupted. 'No horses, right?'

The girls laughed. 'Actually,' Chrissie's mother said, 'there's the Claremont Riding Academy right off Central Park.'

'In the city? Really?' Lucy asked. 'Where do people ride? The only horses I've ever seen here are pulling carriages or being ridden by police officers.'

'People go riding in Central Park, too,' Debbie said. 'But imagine what it would be like to go riding in the streets! It can't be very much fun with all these cars, buses, and people,' she said, looking around. 'Hey, look, there's a horse-drawn carriage now!'

'It's so pretty, with those pink satin seats,' Carla said.

Lucy sighed. 'And look at that couple. They seem so in love. I wouldn't mind doing that one day.'

Chrissie watched the horse pull the carriage into Central Park, and felt bad for him. He was working hard, and he didn't look very happy about it. How could her friends even think about the gaudy carriage or the couple's romance? That poor horse belonged in a field, not on some dirty city street. He had no fresh grass for grazing – only a bucket of dry oats. Chrissie suddenly had an urge to take him home with her to the farm. She wanted to show him that horse life wasn't always so rotten.

Mrs. Williams had reserved a table ahead of time, so when they got to Rumplemayer's they were seated right away. After they'd each had a light snack, Chrissie turned to her mother. 'Thanks, Mum. I'm having a fabulous time. This is a great birthday party.'

'Yeah, thanks, Mrs. Williams,' Carla put in. 'This was such a neat idea.'

'Today's been perfect . . . even though we didn't do any shopping,' Debbie added.

The girls laughed but stopped quickly when they caught sight of the waiter coming towards the table with a gigantic hot-fudge sundae topped with a lit candle. Chrissie couldn't imagine anything more luscious even in her wildest fantasies.

'Wow!' Debbie exclaimed.

'That's almost obscene,' Carla added. 'How are we going to eat that whole thing?'

The waiter set it down in front of Chrissie, and her friends began to sing 'Happy Birthday' to her. Then the waiter and the people at the next table joined in.

By the time they finished singing, Chrissie had turned bright red.

'Make a wish,' Debbie whispered, squeezing Chrissie's knee under the table.

Chrissie closed her eyes and imagined Outstanding as a grown horse, tall and handsome. She was wearing a black velvet riding habit and leading him into the ring at the hunter-jumper show. And in her fantasy, she was almost as tall as he was.

But then she remembered that no matter how much she loved him, she would have to let him go at the end-of-the-year auction. *Don't get attached*, she warned herself as the picture dissolved from her mind. *Remember the number one rule.*

She blew out the candle and everyone applauded. Chrissie smiled weakly and sat back in her chair so suddenly that she almost tipped over. Then Debbie poked her in the ribs. 'So, what did you wish for?'

With her mouth full of hot fudge and whipped cream, Chrissie looked at her friend.

'You know I can't tell,' she mumbled. 'If I do, then my wish won't come true.'

'Oh, come on . . . tell us,' Carla pressed.

'Yeah,' Lucy said. 'It's no fun if you don't share your wish. How will we know if it comes true or not if you don't tell us?'

Chrissie thought for a moment. 'Sorry,' she said finally. 'You'll just have to wait and see.'

'Figures!' said Debbie.

'Eat up, girls,' Chrissie's mother said, looking at her watch. 'We have to start heading back before it gets too dark.'

By the time they reached Williams Farm, it was almost seven o'clock. Mr. Williams, Mr. Patterson, and the grooms were just finishing up at the barn. David was putting the final touches on Chrissie's traditional birthday barbecue, cooked out in the shed and served up inside. Chrissie loved barbecued food, and though her birthday was in February, her mother always prepared whatever Chrissie wanted in honour of the special day. French fries and beans and barbecued hamburgers and hot dogs was usually what Chrissie requested.

'Hey, David,' Debbie said as soon as they got in the door. 'Need some help?'

Chrissie rolled her eyes. Debbie was flirting with her brother again. Well, at least they'd eat sooner with two people setting up, and then they could get to the part Chrissie had been waiting for her whole life.

After everyone had eaten until they were ready to burst, David and Debbie helped drag Chrissie's presents into the family room. Chrissie got a lot of presents she really liked – horse posters, a horse-magazine subscription from her friends, a new pair of paddock boots from her brother, and a book on horse care from Dr. Anderson. The inscription inside the book read:

To Chrissie,
On your thirteenth birthday. From one
horse lover to another.

Judith Anderson

Finally, all the presents had been opened, and Chrissie was surrounded by empty boxes, wrapping paper, and ribbons. The big present, Chrissie knew, was still to come. A horse of her own – that's what she really wanted this year. These wonderful gifts would have satisfied her completely the year before, but she felt differently now. She felt like a real adult – she actually wanted the responsibility of caring for a horse.

'Well, Chrissie, looks like you got quite a haul this year,' her father said with a mischievous smile. He knew what Chrissie was waiting for.

Chrissie just smiled and began chewing on her fingernail nervously.

Her mother looked at her. 'Go ahead, Bob,' she said to Chrissie's father. 'You'd better go ahead and do it before she bursts!'

'All right, Chrissie, I guess it's time.' Mr. Williams cleared his throat and turned towards his daughter. 'As you know, this is a tradition that was started by your grandfather over thirty years ago, when I turned thirteen and got my first foal to raise. Your brother got his own foal, too, when he turned thirteen. And now that you're thirteen, you've earned the right to raise your own foal.' He paused and thought for a moment. 'When you and David have children, I hope you will carry on this tradition.'

Her father then rose to his feet. 'Come on outside, Chrissie. Something very special is waiting for you.'

Her horse was waiting for her! Chrissie couldn't believe that after all the years she'd spent waiting, the big moment was finally here. She was sure everyone in the room could hear her heart pounding in her chest.

Debbie, Carla, and Lucy came up to Chrissie and gave her a big hug. They knew how important this occasion was for her.

She followed her mother and father as they made their way outside and over to the corral. Chrissie heard her friends giggling and talking

64

close behind her, but she had no thoughts of anything except what lay ahead. After weeks of dreaming about what it would be like to care for Outstanding, the time had finally come. She realised now that she'd thought of little else since the day the colt was born.

But now she'd really have to get serious. Her dreams were about to become reality – she'd have to work harder than she ever had in her life. But she knew she was up to the challenge.

I've got to be the luckiest person in the world, Chrissie thought as she and her family walked toward the corral in what seemed like slow motion. *It just doesn't get better than this.*

But when Chrissie got to the gate of the corral, she froze. *What's* that *horse doing here?* she wondered. Unable to speak, she looked from her father's smiling face to her mother's, and then to David. In the corral stood a gangly, gawky colt with a big red bow tied around his neck. His legs were way too long for his body, and he looked unsure on his feet. He stepped sideways, as if he was trying to steady himself, then tripped and almost fell. Watching him struggle to remain standing was more than Chrissie could bear.

'Where – where's Outstanding?' Chrissie finally stammered. 'Where is he?' She looked around wildly, turning in a circle, searching for her favourite foal. She nearly lost her footing herself. But it was useless. Outstanding wasn't there.

Then the shock began to fade and Chrissie realised what was going on. She'd practically forgotten about him, but the colt that stood in the corral waiting for her to untie him and take care of him for a whole entire year was Squire's Boy, the chestnut Anglo-Arab foal.

'Outstanding isn't going to be my horse?' Chrissie asked, looking at both her parents. Then tears began to form in her eyes before they could answer. She already knew what they were going to say, and her disappointment was crushing.

Chrissie could see that her friends were beginning to look uncomfortable, but she couldn't help herself. She couldn't pretend to be pleased when she wasn't. She felt like someone had kicked her in the stomach.

Her father came over and put his arm around her. 'Now listen, Chrissie,' he said in a low voice, so that only she could hear. 'No one ever said you were going to raise Outstanding. Your mother and I know that you love Outstanding, but we've also noticed that you've been treating him like a pet, not like a valuable foal to be raised in the same way as all the other foals.'

She tried to pull away from her father, but he held her firmly by the shoulders and made her listen.

'You have to learn, Chrissie, that all the foals are equally important to the farm, and they all deserve your love and attention.'

Chrissie tried her hardest to understand what her father was telling her, but she couldn't help feeling that it was all so unfair. Then she felt her mother's gentle touch on her arm.

'We trust you so completely,' her mother said, 'that we want you to raise the first Anglo-Arab bred from two of our own horses.'

Chrissie just looked at her mother. Didn't she understand what Outstanding meant to her?

'Chrissie,' her mother went on in a gentle tone, 'there wouldn't be much challenge for you in raising Outstanding. We all know *he's* going to be great. Besides, Squire's Boy is a smaller foal and he'll be much easier for you to handle.'

Chrissie took a deep breath. She didn't want to seem spoiled or unreasonable, but she had to tell her parents how she felt. She would have to take care of this foal for a whole year, and she honestly couldn't care less about him!

'Mum, Dad, I really want my own horse, but I don't want to raise Squire's Boy,' she said, trying to sound mature and rational. 'Just look at him. He's such a klutz! His legs are too long, and he still can't run as well as the other foals. There may even be something wrong with him – he looks as if he's having trouble just standing. And besides, I really had my heart set on raising Outstanding.'

67

Chrissie held her breath. This was it. What her parents said now determined what the next year would hold for her.

Finally her father spoke, his tone kind but firm. 'I'm sorry, but we've made up our minds, Chrissie. Either you raise Squire's Boy or you raise no horse at all. Now, what's it going to be?'

Then David pulled Chrissie aside. 'Come on,' he whispered in her ear. 'It's only a horse, and you're only going to be stuck with him for ten months. You can do that, can't you?'

Her brother was right, Chrissie realised. She could take care of the colt for ten months, then buy a show jumper at the end of the year with the money she made from the auction. That wouldn't be too difficult, she decided.

'Okay,' she said to her parents, 'I'll raise him.' She attempted a smile. 'And I'm sorry if I sounded ungrateful. I was just a little surprised, that's all.'

'That's my girl!' Her father hugged her and gave her a kiss on the cheek.

'All right, everyone. Let's go back to the house for some birthday cake,' Chrissie's mother called out. 'That is, if any of you have any room left after all we've eaten today!'

'I'll be right in, Mum,' Chrissie said as she went over to examine her new charge. David and Mr. Williams went into the house with

Chrissie's mother, but Debbie, Lucy and Carla lingered in the corral for a little while longer.

'He doesn't look that bad, Chrissie,' Lucy pointed out.

'Yeah,' Chrissie said sadly as she looked at the colt, 'I guess you're right. Listen, guys, I'll meet you inside, okay? I'd like to bring him back to his stall. Tell my mum I'll be right there.'

Her friends reluctantly walked toward the house, leaving Chrissie standing alone at the corral gate. Debbie turned back and motioned for Chrissie to join them, but she shook her head and waved them on.

Then she forced herself to turn toward the colt. To her surprise, the colt moved closer to her.

'Boy, what a major bummer this turned out to be!' she said to him. 'You'll never be as good a horse as Outstanding, but I guess we're going to have to make the best of a rotten situation.' She took a deep breath and looked down at the little horse. 'But I don't know how I'll ever love you. Outstanding was the horse I really wanted. I never wanted anything so badly.'

She looked down at her feet. All the excitement of her birthday had completely dissipated, and she couldn't help but feel cheated. What was supposed to be the greatest present had turned out to be the biggest letdown. Tears started to flow down her cheeks and Chrissie didn't try to stop them. She leaned against the fence and stared at the colt, wishing he were Outstanding.

After a few minutes, she wiped the wet streaks off her cheeks and walked over to the horse. 'Now, if you and I are going to work together for almost a year, we'd better get the ground rules straight. Just remember, I'm the boss and you're the horse. Understand?'

'Okay, Chrissie!' David said in his best Mr. Ed voice.

Chrissie jumped and angrily turned towards David. 'Don't you ever sneak up on me like that again. I'm really not in the mood for any of your games tonight, David.'

'Oh, I'm sorry, Chrissie,' David said when he saw her red-rimmed eyes. He went to her and draped his arm around her shoulders. 'Listen,' he said, 'I know how much you wanted to raise Outstanding, but this will work out even better for you. Believe me.'

'Oh, sure!' she said sceptically.

'No, I'm serious,' he said.

'What do you mean?'

'You remember Gallant Boy?'

'Sure, the first colt you raised. Why?'

'Well, I never told anyone before, but after he was sold at the auction I used to cry myself to sleep every night for the longest time. I still get sad thinking about him, and it's been almost five years since I last saw him.'

'What does that have to do with me?' Chrissie asked, puzzled.

'Think about it. Would you feel worse if you had to raise Outstanding and see him sold at the auction – or Squire's Boy?'

Chrissie slowly began to understand. David had a point. She wouldn't care when this odd-looking, awkward horse was sold at the auction. In fact, she'd probably even cheer when she sold him. 'You know, maybe you're right,' she said. 'I'll try to get Squire's Boy into shape, and maybe he'll bring in enough money to buy a good jumper.'

'And you know,' David said as he put his foot up on the bottom rail of the fence, 'Mum and Dad meant this as an honour. They think Anglo-Arabs are the future of this farm, and Squire's Boy is really important to them.'

Chrissie threw her arms around her brother's neck and gave him a big kiss.

'Hey, what's that for?' he asked.

'Oh, just for being a big oaf. That's all!'

'Come on, birthday girl, we'd better get back to the celebration before we freeze to death . . . or worse.'

'What could be worse than that?' Chrissie replied.

'Well, your friends could eat all the ice cream and cake and make off with all your presents,'

71

David said with a smile. 'So let me give you a hand putting Squire's Boy back in his stall.'

David opened the corral gate for Chrissie, who had taken the colt by his halter. As she started to walk him out of the corral, the young colt tripped and staggered. Chrissie stopped and looked back at the horse. She smiled faintly and shook her head. 'Nice going, klutz,' she said sarcastically.

'What did you say?' her brother asked.

'I said "klutz," and I just made a decision. If I'm going to be raising this horse for almost a year, then I'm going to give him a new name . . . one that fits him better.' She paused before continuing. 'I'm not going to call him Squire's Boy any more. He doesn't look like a Squire's Boy and he certainly doesn't act like one. From now on his new name is going to be Klutz!'

David slapped his thigh and laughed out loud.

'Seems like the perfect name to me!' he said.

Six

CHRISSIE WAS IN HER ROOM TALKING ON THE PHONE when her brother suddenly burst in.

'Haven't you ever heard of knocking?' she said, covering the mouthpiece of the phone.

'You'd better be quiet and listen to me. You don't know what trouble you're in,' David said. The serious look on his face sent a shiver down her spine.

She removed her hand from the phone. 'Debbie, I have to go,' Chrissie explained before hanging up. Then she turned to her brother. 'All right, what is it?'

'I just came from the barn.'

'So?'

'Well, Dad and I were walking by Klutz's stall, and Dad had a fit!'

'Uh-oh!' Chrissie could feel the blood

73

slowly drain from her face.

'Yeah, uh-oh is right,' her brother continued. 'Dad saw Klutz standing in the middle of a filthy stall and lost it! There was no water, no feed, and his coat was dirty.'

'What did Dad say?'

'Well, he counted to ten very slowly.'

'Oh, David!' she moaned. 'What else happened?'

'Nothing. He just turned around and stomped away. He had to give Mr. Patterson a new feed list, but he should be here any minute now.'

Chrissie's hand flew up to her mouth. 'Oh no!'

'Oh yes. And I'm not sticking around for the fireworks. I just came by to warn you.'

Just then the back door slammed.

'Later,' David said as he ducked out of her room.

Chrissie's heart was pounding as she waited for her father. She knew that he was going to be furious with her.

As hard as she tried, the truth was that Chrissie couldn't get excited about working with Klutz and his dam, Teacup. And recently it had been even more difficult to get her chores done. It was late in April, and summer holiday was only six weeks away. Chrissie had never had such a bad case of spring fever before.

On more than one occasion, when she was

supposed to be grooming Klutz or mucking out his stall, she had drifted over to Outstanding's stall, just to see him. She couldn't help but notice that the colt was turning into a miniature Excellence. He was developing beautiful lines, and he radiated a certain confidence and power that comes with being a true champion. By contrast, Klutz was . . . well, a klutz. Chrissie longed to be training Outstanding.

Chrissie had also learned that raising a foal was more work than she'd thought it would be. Not only did she have to muck out Klutz and Teacup's stall every morning and evening, she also had to feed, water, groom, and exercise the colt daily, even on the rainiest days. All of her clothing seemed to be permanently mud-stained, but that wasn't half as bad as sloshing around in the mud in the hard-driving rain.

Sometimes Chrissie rushed through all the things she needed to do for her colt, and she often ended up doing a sloppy job. Her father had noticed her negligence, but he'd barely said a word to her about it. Instead, he'd said, 'If the horse could take care of himself, anyone could raise him.'

David had covered for her a couple of times when she had neglected Klutz in favour of riding Tuskers or spending time with Debbie. But he couldn't cover for her all the time, and Chrissie knew she was pushing her luck. Her parents couldn't ignore her irresponsible behaviour much longer. Running the farm was a business and there was, after all, a life at stake – Klutz's.

Her father's heavy footsteps jolted Chrissie out of her reverie. She heard her father pause for a moment when he got to her door. Then he knocked.

'Come on in,' Chrissie said, scrambling around to make it look as if she were dressing for an afternoon at the barn.

Her father stepped into the room. Chrissie couldn't help thinking that he seemed much taller and more imposing than usual.

'Hi, Dad,' Chrissie said casually as she pulled on her heavy white socks and thrust her feet into a pair of boots. 'I wish I could stick around and talk, but I've got to run now.' She grabbed her jacket and headed toward the door. 'Klutz is waiting. And when duty calls . . .'

Her cheerful voice trailed off as her father planted a firm hand on her shoulder, stopping her in her tracks. She was so scared she didn't dare move. 'I understand you were making plans with Debbie for tonight's dance?'

'Uh, yeah. It's the big spring dance at the junior high. Debbie and I are meeting Lucy and Carla there,' she explained.

'Sounds great.'

'Yeah, I even got this really neat dress for it.

It's blue, with thin straps. Want to see it?'

'Maybe later. When does the dance start?'

Chrissie slowly let out her breath. Her father wasn't so mad after all – he just wanted to make sure she had enough time to care for Klutz before she went out. David had made a big deal out of nothing and scared her half to death!

'I'm supposed to be at Debbie's at five forty-five,' Chrissie answered finally. 'David said he would drive me over after he finishes his chores. Is that all right?'

'Hmmm. David still has chores to do? It's too bad he isn't as fast as some people I know,' Mr. Williams said.

Chrissie was about to tell him that she wasn't finished yet and that she'd like to go get started right away, but he went on before she could get a word in.

'I was at the barn a little while ago, and I just checked on Squire's Boy. That was,' he said, stopping to look at his watch, 'exactly fifteen minutes ago. And do you know what? Both the horse and the stall were filthy. And I'll bet he hasn't been exercised, either.' Her father crossed his arms over his chest and looked down at her. Chrissie didn't dare speak. 'Now, according to my calculations,' he continued, 'it takes at least three hours to bathe, groom, exercise, feed, and water a horse, and that doesn't include cleaning out his stall. Obviously, you've got some new,

77

superfast system that allows you to wait until you're ready to party before you have to do your chores.'

'Dad, I'm sorry. I was just getting ready to go down and do those things now. I was busy before, and I forgot about Klutz.'

'Well, I'm happy to know you still remember your horse's name,' her father said as he watched Chrissie dash around the room searching for her jacket and gloves.

'Dad, look . . . I know I've forgotten about Klutz before, but this will be the last time. I promise! So do you think I could get one of the grooms to give me a hand just this once?'

'Sorry, Chrissie. They all have their own responsibilities to attend to.'

'Well, then, how about one of the hands? A couple of them are really good with Klutz. And I know they wouldn't mind helping me. Maybe one of them can muck out Klutz's stall while I exercise him.'

'No, Chrissie, the hands will be off in an hour, and I'm sure they still have a lot to do.'

Chrissie felt herself beginning to sweat. 'How about David, then? I know he'll help me.'

'Nope! Not this time, kiddo. David's got a date tonight. That's why he offered to drop you off. It's on the way to Michelle's.'

Chrissie couldn't think of any other solution, so she just stared at her father.

'Well, I guess you're finally going to have to face up to the fact that you blew it,' he said matter-of-factly. 'You know the deal. Klutz is yours, and it's your responsibility to take care of him – by yourself!'

'But if I have to do everything myself, I'll never be ready in time for tonight,' Chrissie said, hating the whine she heard in her voice.

'You had all morning and most of the afternoon to attend to your horse. But instead of doing that, you wasted your time on the phone,' her father said to her unsympathetically. 'So now, I guess, you can't go.'

'But that's not fair!' Chrissie said, clenching her fists. 'I really wanted to go to this dance.'

Her father looked at her incredulously. 'Not fair? Not fair to whom?' he boomed. 'You wanted a horse to raise. It wasn't forced on you. If anyone has a right to complain about life not being fair, it's Klutz. He didn't do anything to deserve the kind of treatment you've given him. Why should *he* suffer?'

Chrissie looked down and began chewing on her fingernails.

Her father went on. 'If you don't want to raise that horse, let me know now, and I'll have one of the grooms take over. But if someone else takes over, you won't receive any of the money he brings in at the auction. *And* you won't get another chance to raise a colt.' He paused. 'It's your choice, Chrissie. But remember, if you want to be treated like an adult, you have to accept all of the responsibilities that go along with it.'

Chrissie sat down on her bed dejectedly.

After a moment, her father sat down next to her and put his arm around her shoulders. 'Listen to me, Chrissie. I'll admit, it's not easy being an adult. We often have to do things we don't want to do . . . Now, your mother and I both think you're a pretty terrific kid. We also know that you can do just about anything if you set your mind to it. That's why we chose Squire's Boy for you to raise.'

'I know, Dad,' Chrissie said slowly. 'I'm sorry I let you down.'

'You didn't let *me* down. You let Klutz down, and even worse, you let yourself down. Chrissie, you have a special gift for handling horses that not many people have. Anyone can raise a Thoroughbred, but raising an Anglo-Arab requires much more patience and understanding.'

Chrissie nodded.

Her father stood up. 'I know raising Klutz isn't easy, but if I didn't think you were up to the challenge, I would have given the colt to someone more experienced. *I know* you can do it, Chrissie. Now, get yourself down to the barn,' he said.

Chrissie looked deep into her father's eyes and felt something stir within her. He was absolutely right. She *had* to rise to the challenge. She couldn't let Klutz down. He didn't deserve to be ignored. She smiled a little. 'I'll be right down. I have to call Debbie and tell her I can't make it to the dance tonight.'

'Look,' her father said with a kind smile, 'how about if I meet you at the stable in five minutes? Maybe we can finish up a little faster.'

'Thanks, Dad,' Chrissie said, feeling better already.

After he had closed the door behind him, she lay back on her bed and thought about everything he had just told her. She really did have to get serious now. Being thirteen meant having real responsibilities and thinking about things other than herself. *From now on,* Chrissie resolved, *Klutz is going to be number one on my priority list – whether I like him or not.*

Seven

FOR THE NEXT TWO MONTHS, CHRISSIE SPENT EVERY spare moment taking care of Klutz. Each morning, she'd muck out the stall he shared with Teacup and make sure he had his feed and water. Then, when she got home from school, she would exercise and groom him before riding Tuskers. And after dinner she'd clean his stall out once more before going to her room and tackling her homework.

The first few days, it took a huge effort to haul herself out of bed at five thirty. It was just so difficult to get motivated for a horse Chrissie didn't even like! But when she thought about the horse she was going to buy with the money from the auction, the work seemed a little more bearable. So by six o'clock every morning, Chrissie was in

Klutz's stall with a pitchfork in hand, changing his straw.

'I'll bet we're the only ones dumb enough to get up this early,' she'd mumble to Klutz as she worked. 'Boy, you really are a pain in the neck!'

A couple of weeks into the routine, however, Chrissie began to get used to devoting her mornings to Klutz. She even got into the habit of telling him her schedule for the day, and sometimes she would study for tests by reciting facts to him. He seemed to have a particular interest in the American Civil War, for some reason.

Then her routine started to change a bit. Instead of rushing off as soon as Klutz's stall was clean, Chrissie would linger a while.

'. . . so Debbie and I are going to study for Mrs. Kipling's English exam at lunch today. I heard it's going to be *really* tough,' Chrissie said to Klutz as she scratched between his ears. 'I don't know how I'm ever going to remember who wrote which poem. We did so many of them!'

Klutz grunted and lowered his head.

'What's the matter, Klutz?' Chrissie asked, still scratching. 'Do you want me to scratch over here?' She moved her hand and rubbed behind his ears.

Klutz whickered with pleasure.

'Oh, you like that, huh? You're such a weird

little horse. Most horses I know like to be scratched *between* the ears, not behind them!'

The long-awaited summer holiday finally began as the last bell of the year rang out its final *clang-clang-clang*. Chrissie and her friends ran out of school yelling and screaming happily.

Chrissie was thrilled at the prospect of having the next three months free, but at the same time, she was sorry that the year had ended. Next Autumn, Lucy and Carla would be attending the new Robert Morris Junior High on the other side of town, while Chrissie and Debbie would be attending Middletown Junior High.

The bus pulled out of the parking lot for the last time that year, and the four girls watched the school building grow smaller in the distance. There were tears in their eyes as they realised they would never make this trip together again.

'It's unbelievable! Eight whole years have gone by since the four of us met in Mrs. Gardner's kindergarten class,' Chrissie said nostalgically. 'Who would have thought this day would ever come?'

'Just think,' Debbie said. 'Next year we'll probably be dating high-school guys.'

Chrissie looked at her friends and smiled. She would miss Carla and Lucy so much. They were her best friends after Debbie, and she had been through so much with them over the years.

'So, when do you two leave for camp?' she said, growing serious.

'Mum and Dad are going to drive me to the Poconos on Sunday,' Carla said with a hint of sadness in her voice. 'They're going to spend the day up there and help me get settled in.'

'My parents are taking me up to camp next weekend,' Lucy said. 'I think this will be my last year there as a camper, though. I want a job as a C.I.T. next year.'

Debbie stared at Lucy in mock disbelief. 'They'd really let you be a counsellor-in-training, knowing how weird you are?' she said with a straight face.

Lucy opened and closed her mouth several times, but nothing came out. Then everyone burst out laughing.

'What are *you* laughing at, Carla?' Lucy snapped. 'You can't be a C.I.T. at your camp till you're at least fifteen,' she said smugly

'I don't want to be a C.I.T., anyway,' Carla shot back. 'In fact, this is my last year at camp. Mum says I can stay home and baby-sit for the neighbours next year, and I can use the money I make for clothes and make-up and stuff.'

As the bus approached Williams Farm, Chrissie turned to Debbie. 'So, how about coming over tomorrow? I have a lot of work to do with Klutz, but we could go horseback riding afterward.'

'I'd love to come over and hang out with you and the Klutz-meister, Chrissie,' Debbie replied. 'But I'm going to be spending all summer baby-sitting my little brother, so tomorrow I'm going on a shopping expedition. It may be my last chance.' She shifted in her seat to face Chrissie. 'Hey, why don't you come along?'

'Sorry,' Chrissie replied, 'but I can't. I have too many things to do around the farm, and I'll get in big trouble if I neglect Klutz again.'

Debbie sighed. 'Oh. Well, maybe next time, okay?'

Suddenly Chrissie's face lit up. 'Hey, why don't we have a sleepover? We haven't done that in a long time, and this will be the last time we'll all be together till Carla and Lucy get back from camp. What do you say?'

'Yeah.'

'Great.'

'All right!' Everyone answered at once.

When the bus stopped in front of Williams Farm, Chrissie got up to leave. 'Call me as soon as you get home and let me know about tonight,' she told her friends. 'I'll make sure we have enough food to last until morning. Any requests?'

'Yeah, have your mum make her special fried chicken,' said Lucy.

86

'And how about corn muffins and apple pie with ice cream?' Carla added.

Debbie licked her lips. 'Maybe she could whip up a batch of sausage and peppers, too.'

'You got it!' Chrissie said, getting off the bus. 'Peanut butter and jelly sandwiches for everyone. And s'mores for dessert!' She waved good-bye to her friends, then headed up the road to the house. She was so excited about the sleepover that she ran all the way home and burst in through the front door. 'Mum! Mum! Where are you?'

'In the kitchen. What's wrong?'

Chrissie hurried into the kitchen and found her mother putting two pies in the oven.

'Apple?' Chrissie asked hopefully.

'Of course!' her mother said as she closed the oven door. 'It's your favourite. I wanted to make you a special dessert to celebrate the last day of school.'

Chrissie threw her arms around her mother's neck and kissed her on the cheek. 'Thanks, Mum. You're super!' she said, moving over to the counter to clean up the mess of flour and dough.

Her mother stood by and watched her clean. After a couple of minutes, she asked, 'So what is it, Chrissie?'

'What do you mean, what is it? I'm just helping you out a little. That's all,' Chrissie responded.

'Come on, Chrissie,' her mother said knowingly 'Let's hear it.'

'All right,' Chrissie said finally. 'I just wondered if I could have Debbie, Lucy, and Carla over for the night.'

Her mother looked at her and smiled. 'Sure! That's a great idea. Just make sure all your chores are done before they arrive.'

'Yeah, okay. And is it all right if I tell them to come over around six thirty?'

'Of course. Now go and get started on your chores.'

Chrissie kissed her mother on the cheek again before running up to her room and changing out of her school clothes. Ten minutes later, Chrissie was on her way to Klutz's stall.

'Hi, boy,' Chrissie said as she approached her horse. 'And hello, Teacup.' Klutz's dam was standing in one corner with her face in her feed bucket. 'You get a treat today because it's the last day of school. Besides, I think you deserve something for helping me get through finals in one piece.'

Chrissie reached into her pocket for some sugar cubes and held them out for Klutz to eat.

The colt gobbled up the cubes as if they were the last pieces of sugar on earth, making funny slurping noises. Chrissie laughed and patted his neck. 'You may not be the most perfect horse I've ever seen, but you *are* unique,' she said affectionately. She went over to the grooming kit in the corner of the stall and took out the two brushes she used on Klutz's coat. Then, starting at the neck and working her way back, she carefully began grooming him.

By the time she had finished, Klutz's chestnut coat gleamed in the light. Chrissie stepped back to admire her handiwork. She couldn't get over how much he had changed in just four months. He had lost some of his awkwardness. He seemed to be growing into his long legs and he looked almost proportional. *He may just turn out to be a beautiful animal one day*, Chrissie realised. *Who would ever have thought it possible?*

There was a sudden clatter of hoofs right outside Klutz's stall just then, and Chrissie poked her head out to see what was going on. She caught a glimpse of Outstanding being led past and immediately felt her optimism fade. She sighed. He looked stronger and more beautiful than ever. 'You look better every day, Klutz, but you're still no Outstanding,' she told the colt. 'But I guess that's life!'

After grooming Klutz, Chrissie mucked out his stall and filled his feed and water buckets. She put away her tools and gave Klutz one last pat on the neck. Then Chrissie saddled up Tuskers for her daily ride.

When Chrissie returned from the stable, her

mother told her that Debbie had called to say all three of them were allowed to spend the night. After Chrissie and her mother had made sure that the girls had plenty of pillows and blankets for the night, David offered to take Chrissie to the supermarket for some popcorn and marshmallows.

As they were waiting in line to pay for their purchases, David turned to her.

'Now that you're finished with school for the summer, there's going to be a lot more pressure on you,' he told Chrissie. 'For the next twelve weeks you're really going to have to buckle down and take care of Klutz. I won't be there to bail you out any more, you know.'

'What do you mean? Where are you going?'

'Chrissie, I told you. I'm going to be an instructor at a riding camp in the Catskills. Don't you listen when I tell you stuff?'

'I don't think you ever told me,' Chrissie said. 'But does this mean you won't be there when I show Tuskers in the hunter-jumper show?'

'I guess not. I'll be leaving next week and won't be back till the end of August.' David took out his wallet as the check-out girl finished adding up the groceries.

'Well, I guess that means I get to be an only child sooner than I thought,' Chrissie said as they walked out of the supermarket. 'Just what I've always wanted!'

David looked at her and smiled. 'Yeah. I'll miss you too, shrimp.'

Chrissie was silent the entire way home. In spite of his non-stop teasing, Chrissie knew she would miss her brother.

By the time Chrissie's friends arrived, she and her mother had a large tray of sandwiches already made. The girls helped carry the food up to Chrissie's room, and by seven o'clock the four girls were settled in for the night with food, pop, fashion magazines, and make-up.

As they thumbed through the latest issue of *Seventeen*, trying to find the newest hairdos and make-up tricks, Chrissie noticed that Debbie seemed preoccupied. She scooted over to her best friend and said, 'Hey, what's the problem? Run out of words?'

Instead of laughing, Debbie started to cry.

Chrissie and the other two girls immediately huddled around Debbie and tried to console her. Chrissie didn't know why Debbie was crying, but she knew the problem had to be major, because *nobody* cried on the last day of school!

Finally Debbie calmed down enough to talk. 'My mum told me on the way over here tonight that she's accepted a new job.'

'Hey, that's great!' Chrissie said, trying to ease the tension. 'What's so bad about that?'

'It's in Los Angeles. I have to move to

California in two weeks!' Debbie said, her tears flowing over again.

'What?' Chrissie said in shock.

Debbie looked at her and nodded her head. 'It's true,' she said, sobbing. 'I'm really leaving.'

Chrissie stared at her best friend. She couldn't believe it! Her best friend in the whole world was abandoning her forever, and Carla and Lucy were going to be away at camp for the entire summer. Then it dawned on her that not only would she be alone this summer, but Carla and Lucy would be attending a different junior high school in the fall.

'But why? Why?' Chrissie stammered. 'Why does she have to go all the way out there for a new job? It's just not fair,' she managed to say. Then Chrissie put her arms around Debbie and started crying, too.

When Mrs. Williams came by to check on them a little later, she found all four of them red-eyed and sitting on Chrissie's bed. She sat down on the bed with the girls and waited until they were ready to tell her what was going on. Before long, Chrissie spoke up and told her mother the sad news.

Mrs. Williams sighed and looked at the girls. 'I'm sorry to hear that, and I wish there were something I could do. It sounds like your mother's career is really taking off, Debbie. And when that happens, sometimes it's necessary to move far away from friends.' She paused. 'But don't look so sad,' she said. 'You can call and write, and you can even visit one another sometimes. It's not as if you girls are going to be living in different galaxies or anything. And you'll always be welcome here when you want to visit, Debbie.'

Chrissie looked at her mother's gentle face and felt a tiny bit better. But Carla, Lucy, and Debbie still seemed very upset, so Chrissie jumped off the bed, and in the most cheerful voice she could muster, said, 'Okay, who's ready for the s'mores?'

The girls immediately perked up. 'That's exactly what we need,' Lucy said, getting up. 'I'm ready!'

By the time they had finished gorging themselves on junk food, it was after midnight. Carla and Lucy curled up in their sleeping bags and went to sleep, but Chrissie and Debbie stayed up a little longer to talk.

'I still can't believe I'm moving to California,' Debbie said, brushing her hair out of her eyes. 'I mean, even though I'll miss you a lot, I guess it'll be pretty cool. I'll probably see a whole bunch of movie stars. Maybe I'll even be discovered by a famous producer.'

Chrissie couldn't work up any enthusiasm. 'But what am I going to do without you?' she said sadly. 'You're the only person I can really talk to.'

'Well, you still have Klutz,' Debbie replied.

'Klutz? Are you kidding? Klutz is just a horse. No way! It'll never be the same.' Chrissie stared at her best friend. She had just begun to realise how soon she would be leaving. 'You know,' she whispered hoarsely, 'David's going away for the summer, too, and now you're leaving forever.'

'Hey,' Debbie said, trying to sound upbeat, 'David will be back before you know it. And, like your mum said, you can come out to California for a visit, and I'll come back to Middletown. Besides, we'll talk every day on the phone. It'll be just like I never left.'

'Yeah, I guess we can work it out somehow. But David's leaving for college right after he gets back at the end of the summer,' Chrissie said as she crawled under her covers.

Debbie slid into her sleeping bag. 'Oh, that's right. Well, look on the bright side – at least he won't be around to bug you anymore,' she said, yawning. 'Good night, Chrissie.'

'Good night,' Chrissie replied. But for a long time after, Chrissie stared up at the ceiling, feeling the lump in her throat grow bigger and bigger. It seemed as if everyone was leaving her behind.

As soon as she heard Debbie's steady

breathing and knew she was asleep, Chrissie turned her face into her pillow and let her tears flow freely. What a way to start the summer holiday! It just didn't seem possible. How in the world could anyone expect her to go on without her best friend?

Chrissie tossed and turned for a while, then decided to put on her boots and take a walk to the barn. She figured that by the time she got back, she'd be tired enough to fall asleep. On the way to the barn she couldn't help but marvel at the perfectly clear night sky. The full moon and glittering stars cheered her up.

Quietly she crept into the barn so as not to wake the sleeping horses. Of course, Klutz was sleeping like a baby, snuggled up against Teacup. He slept like he didn't have a care in the world, and Chrissie wondered for a moment what it would be like to be a horse and not have to worry about school and friends and dealing with life in general.

Suddenly Chrissie heard a high-pitched noise. It was an awful sound, like an animal in pain. She wheeled around and walked back down the barn aisle until she found the horse who'd been making the noise. It was Tuskers. His eyes looked huge in his head, and he was nudging one of his hindlegs with his muzzle. When he saw her, he stopped making the sound. And he slowly fell asleep as she stroked his leg.

Thank goodness Dr. Anderson is coming tomorrow to check on the foals, Chrissie thought. Something is wrong with Tuskers!

Eight

EARLY THE NEXT MORNING, CHRISSIE WAS STRUGGLING with Klutz in the corral. She was having a terrible time getting him to work on the longe line, the long, heavy rope used to control a horse during training. She was starting to think that training Klutz was going to be the hardest thing she'd ever have to do in her life, and she wondered whether or not her efforts were ever going to amount to anything. And worrying about Tuskers wasn't helping her concentrate one bit.

After she had said good-bye to all her friends that morning, Chrissie reported Tuskers's strange behaviour to her father. He assured her that he'd have Dr. Anderson look at the old horse as soon as she arrived, and he also told Chrissie to prepare herself for the worst. Tuskers wasn't a young horse, and if he was injured or in very bad pain, he might have to be put out of his misery.

Chrissie tried not to think about Tuskers while Klutz was at the end of the longe line, but she was getting more and more frustrated as the minutes went by. For what seemed like the hundredth time, Chrissie gave her colt the command to trot around her in a circle. They had the walk part down pretty well, but when Chrissie cracked the long whip to urge Klutz into a trot, he moved forward for only a few strides, and then he came trotting over to Chrissie.

'Klutz, no!' Chrissie knew that shouting at the horse was pointless, but it relieved her frustrations, if nothing else. 'Let's try it again, Klutz.'

They worked for twenty minutes more before Chrissie finally gave up. Klutz was a little too young to be longed anyway, Chrissie knew, but she didn't think it would hurt to get him used to the feel of the longe line. Afterwards Chrissie jotted down Klutz's progress in his daily log, along with his height, weight, feed allotment, and general physical condition.

' . . . and in the last week he's grown almost an inch. He's now nine and a half hands tall,' she reported to her parents at lunchtime.

'That's fine, Chrissie,' her father commented

as he leaned back in his chair. 'Though it's hard to tell who'll grow more this summer, you or Klutz.'

Both her parents smiled as Chrissie began turning red. She was pleased about the changes in Klutz, but she found her own body's changes a bit embarrassing. She'd noticed that her jeans seemed to be getting too tight and too short.

'Don't worry, dear,' her mother said. 'We'll be going into the city to get you new school clothes for the autumn as soon as there's a sale.'

Chrissie gave her mother a look that meant business. 'Listen, I really have too much work to do with Klutz to take the time to go shopping. And what if it turns out that something's wrong with Tuskers? The hunter-jumper show is coming up really soon.'

'But your clothes don't fit, Chrissie. You've outgrown them.'

Chrissie grinned. 'Well, I guess there's one reason to be happy that Debbie's moving away. She told me that I could have all her old clothes. She's getting new stuff when she gets to California. So I won't have to go shopping for a year – maybe longer!'

Mrs. Williams smiled. 'I'll let you off the hook this time, but even Debbie's clothes won't fit forever.'

Dr. Anderson finally arrived at the farm at four o'clock. The afternoon training session with

Klutz had been a total waste of time – Chrissie was much too worried about Tuskers to deal with her problem horse.

After a quick examination, Dr. Anderson gave Chrissie and her father the sad news.

'I'm afraid Tuskers won't make it to the hunter-jumper show this year. He's got arthritis, and his days as a show horse are over, Chrissie.'

'Oh, that's terrible,' Chrissie whispered.

The doctor went on. 'It's still in its early stages, but I think because of his age it would be best to put him out to pasture. No more riding for him, or else he'll go lame.'

'We'll let him rest,' Chrissie's father said decisively.

'He should still have some light exercise every day, though,' Dr. Anderson said. 'And as long as you're careful with him, he'll have a very peaceful retirement.'

Chrissie had to force herself not to cry. How could she ever become a vet, a trainer, or a breeder if she got so emotionally involved with the horses? But poor Tuskers! She'd never be able to take him out riding again. Taking a deep breath, Chrissie swallowed back the tears.

Dr. Anderson gave Tuskers a shot to ease the pain, and then she rubbed the horse between the ears until he fell into a deep sleep. 'Come, Chrissie, let's go have a look at Klutz now.'

Chrissie didn't want to leave Tuskers, but she

led the vet to Klutz's stall. Her father had already left them to go back to work.

'My goodness, you've done wonders with him,' the vet said when she saw the colt. 'I can hardly believe that this is the same animal I helped deliver just five months ago. You may very well become a veterinarian one day, Chrissie.'

Chrissie beamed. She always liked getting compliments, but she really respected Dr. Anderson's opinion.

'Thanks, Doc. He *is* turning out okay after all, isn't he?'

'He certainly is,' the doctor responded.

After a moment Dr. Anderson walked over to the colt and began her examination. She checked Klutz's eyes, ears, and teeth, and felt around his neck before working her way towards his hindquarters. The exam took about twenty-five minutes. When she was finished, she went over to her bag and took out a small black case containing hypodermic needles and syringes. Then she drew a blood sample that she would send to a lab and have analysed. Chrissie always hated this part of the exam. *She* didn't like getting shots, so she suspected Klutz and the other horses felt the same way.

Dr. Anderson saw Chrissie wince when she stuck another needle into Klutz's side. 'Don't worry. Klutz hardly feels it,' she said, smiling.

101

Chrissie returned her smile, though she wasn't convinced.

When Dr. Anderson finally finished giving Klutz all his shots, she rewarded him with a handful of apple chunks. 'Here you are, Klutz,' she said fondly. 'You're a good boy, aren't you?' Then Dr. Anderson turned toward Chrissie and slowly shook her head. 'Well, it's exactly as I thought. . .'

Chrissie's heart skipped a beat. *Oh, no. What's wrong with Klutz?* she wondered.

'Your horse is perfect,' the doctor concluded with a broad smile.

Chrissie felt herself breathe again as the doctor's words sank in.

'You've proven me right. This Anglo-Arab is going to make your family's farm famous.' With those words, Dr. Anderson closed her bag and started walking out of the stall. Then she stopped and turned to Chrissie.

'You know, you're really going to make a great vet someday. You like working around animals, and you have a special way with them,' she said.

'Maybe when I graduate from college I could become your assistant,' Chrissie said, her hope rising as she thought of the possibilities.

'Maybe. Of course, you'll have to keep those grades up. It's not easy to get into veterinary school. If you don't get all A's, you're going to have a really hard time finding a school that will accept you.'

Chrissie frowned. *I'd better start paying more attention in my science classes,* she said to herself.

'Don't worry. I know you can do it, Chrissie,' Dr. Anderson assured her. 'I'll even give you a hand with your homework if you need it. Fair enough?'

'Fair enough!' Chrissie responded happily.

Dr. Anderson looked at her watch. 'Well, it's getting late. I'd better hurry and see the other foals. See you later, Chrissie. Bye-bye, Klutz!' The vet gave the horse a final pat on the rump and headed down the barn aisle.

Chrissie watched Dr. Anderson walk out of sight before turning back to her horse. 'All right, you . . . what do you think this is, some kind of holiday? Just because the vet thinks you're gorgeous doesn't mean you can get away with murder,' she said playfully. She took hold of his halter and moved her face right in front of his so that their noses touched. Then Klutz sneezed.

'Gross!' Chrissie said as she jumped back and wiped off her face. 'Boy, you can be pretty disgusting!'

Chrissie went over to get some carrots from a barrel outside Klutz's stall.

'You know,' she said thoughtfully as she fed them to him and Teacup, 'I think you deserve a reward for a good checkup. You actually behaved during Dr. Anderson's visit. It's too bad you don't do the same for our ever-so-exciting workout sessions. Let's see, what can I get you?' Chrissie mused. 'Hey, I know! How would you like a personalised name plate for your halter?'

Klutz snorted and, finding that the carrots were all gone, began munching a mouthful of hay.

'What should it say? Squire's Boy? No! Too formal. Klutz? Nope! Too informal. How about My Klutz?' Chrissie looked at her colt. 'No arguments? Okay, then, that's settled. My Klutz it is!'

Chrissie used the phone in the barn to call Miller's, a tack store in New York City, to order the plate.

'Okay. So you can have it ready in a week? ... Great. How much will it be? ... Fine. Bill it to Williams Farm. We have an account with you. Thanks!' Chrissie hung up the phone and headed back to the house.

'Oh, Mum,' Chrissie said when she found her mother in the family room, 'I ordered a personalised halter plate for Klutz from Miller's. I'm going to use my allowance money to pay you back when the bill comes. Is that okay?'

'That's fine, dear,' Mrs. Williams said. 'What name are you going to have put on the plate – Klutz or Squire's Boy?'

'My Klutz,' said Chrissie. 'Isn't that perfect?'

'My Klutz,' Mrs. Williams repeated with a concerned look on her face.

'What's the matter? Don't you like it?' Chrissie asked.

'It isn't that I don't like it, honey,' her mother began. 'It's just that . . . well, you're going to have to sell Klutz at the December auction. That's only six months away. You know he's not really your Klutz. You have to remember that it's going to be tough for you to sell him, especially if you become attached to him now.'

'Mum, you don't get it!' Chrissie exclaimed. 'I just thought he deserved a reward for having a good exam, that's all. I'm not attached to him, believe me.'

Mrs. Williams sighed. 'Okay. As long as you keep in mind rule number one for horse breeders . . .'

'I know, I know,' Chrissie said. 'Don't get attached!'

'What I'm trying to say, Chrissie, is that getting attached is natural,' her mother explained. 'It's not easy to avoid it. You have to be very, very careful.'

'Mum, I don't think I'm going to have any problems. I can't wait to sell Klutz so I can buy a great jumper – especially now that I can't ride Tuskers.'

Her mother just nodded.

'Will you promise me something, Mum?' Chrissie asked in a timid voice.

'Of course, honey, if I can.'

'I want Tuskers to stay here on the farm, even though we can't ride or show him anymore. I think he deserves that. He's been a great show horse. He's won awards ever since I've been showing him, for five whole years!'

'Well, Dr. Anderson seems to think Tuskers will be content grazing on the farm, so there's no need to worry. Your father and I intend to keep him—'

Chrissie didn't let her mother finish her sentence. She ran over to her and enveloped her in a big bear hug.

Nine

'WE'LL TAKE IT VERY SLOW TODAY, BOY,' CHRISSIE SAID as she led Klutz out of his stall for his morning exercise. It was a particularly hot summer day, and the humidity made it difficult to move. Even Klutz seemed a little bit uncomfortable and sluggish.

As she walked down the aisle she passed Mr. Patterson, who was talking to one of the grooms.

'I don't think I can remember July ever being this hot,' Mr. Patterson said, wiping his forehead. Mr. Patterson liked to check on the horses himself every morning and afternoon to monitor their progress.

'It's only nine thirty and the temperature's already ninety degrees. Today's going to be a real scorcher, so make sure you tell the hands to give the horses extra water and take it easy on the exercise today,' continued Mr. Patterson. 'Also, tell the other grooms they should hose down the mares and young ones before lunch. That should make them a lot more comfortable.'

'Sure thing, Mr. Patterson,' the groom replied.

'Morning, Chrissie,' Mr. Patterson said, coming over to her. 'How's the weaning going?'

Chrissie had been trying to wean Klutz from his mother for the last two weeks, and it hadn't been too difficult. She had to get him to stop nursing from Teacup so that he would eat only solid foods like hay, pellets, and oats. For the first couple of days of the weaning, Chrissie had kept the colt away from his mother for only two or three hours, and she was increasing the time gradually.

'He's doing just fine,' Chrissie replied. 'We're on our way out to the corral for some light exercise, and then I'm going to take him for a swim in the tank.'

'Good idea. If it gets much hotter, I may join you,' he said. 'Well, I'll see you around later.' Then he headed off to finish inspecting the rest of the horses.

Chrissie led Klutz out to the corral and spent the next half hour chasing him in circles and letting him chase her. Older horses received more formal training, but Klutz was still too young to do much more than run and jump around freely. Chrissie sometimes tried exercising him on the longe line, but she knew he wasn't quite ready for more serious work. For now, playing with him was enough to improve his agility and coordination.

By ten o'clock, Chrissie had finished Klutz's workout and had got him into the large tank the Williamses used as the horses' swimming pool.

'Feels good, doesn't it, boy?' she said as Klutz frolicked in the water. 'I sure wish I could come in and join you.'

Klutz seemed to know exactly what Chrissie was saying, because before she knew it, he started splashing around vigorously and shaking himself. Water flew all over the place, completely drenching Chrissie.

'Hey!' Chrissie exclaimed, trying to duck out of the way. 'Take it easy.'

She wiped her face with her T-shirt. 'What are you trying to do, drown me?' The colt bobbed his head up and down as though he were responding, and Chrissie could hardly stop herself from laughing.

As Chrissie watched her colt play in the water she remembered how she used to fantasise about what it would be like to raise her own foal. She knew now that it took a lot more work than she had imagined. And she realised that raising any horse – even one as perfect as Outstanding – was tough. She felt like laughing out loud when she remembered her dreams of what life would be like with Outstanding. What a joke! All horses were work, and Klutz was certainly no exception.

Klutz could really be a pain in the neck sometimes, but Chrissie no longer thought of him as just a dumb horse. He always demanded attention from her in a really funny sort of way, and Chrissie truly enjoyed talking to him, especially since Debbie was in California and David, Lucy, and Carla were away at camp.

She smiled wistfully as she thought about how things had turned out. She hadn't even wanted him at first, and now Klutz was her constant companion. He was like a huge toddler. Chrissie tried to imagine what life would be like with Outstanding instead of Klutz, but she couldn't. Somehow the beautiful Thoroughbred she had dreamed of for so many months seemed far less important to her now. If her father gave her the choice, she wouldn't trade her funny-looking Anglo-Arab for Outstanding, though she'd never admit it to anyone.

Klutz stayed in the cool water for half an hour before Chrissie finally took him back to his stall, where she dried him off and began her favourite task – brushing Klutz's chestnut coat until it shone.

As she picked up the brush and began the

slow, methodical process, Chrissie spoke into his ear.

'This summer has been a total bummer – I mean, apart from spending time with you. You're the only one left I can talk to. You know, you're my only friend now.'

Chrissie stopped brushing for a second and gave her horse a playful pat on the rump. 'Talk about sad. My only friend is a horse!'

Klutz turned his head toward Chrissie and snorted.

'Oh, you have something to say to me, sir?' Chrissie said, stepping closer to the horse's face. 'Okay, I'm listening. What is it?' Chrissie crossed her arms in front of her chest, trying to look as serious as possible.

Klutz moved toward Chrissie and nuzzled her beneath her chin. Then he gave her a shove, sending her sprawling in the hay. Chrissie shook her head to loosen the straw that was clinging to her hair and looked up at her horse. Seeing Klutz's triumphant expression, she burst out laughing.

At that moment, Chrissie's father appeared. 'You all right, Chrissie?' he asked.

Feeling pretty silly, Chrissie lay in the hay with Klutz looming over her. She jumped to her feet and brushed herself off. 'Yes, Dad. I . . . I was just grooming Klutz,' she managed to say.

'Sitting on your bottom like that? That's a

111

strange way of doing it,' he said, laughing. He came into the stall and checked the horse's eyes and teeth. Then he rubbed down the horse's body and began checking his hooves.

When Chrissie's father had finished his inspection, he straightened up and stepped back. Standing with his hands in his back pockets, he studied the animal a while longer before turning to Chrissie. Chrissie thought he had a strange look in his eyes.

'Have you been taking care of this animal?' he asked her.

'Yes, Dad. Why?'

'I mean, all by yourself?'

'Of course,' Chrissie answered, concerned that there might be something wrong.

'Well,' he said as he slowly rubbed his chin with a weathered hand, 'it's just that I'm impressed by the way he looks.'

Chrissie let out a loud sigh of relief.

'You're doing a very fine job with Klutz, Chrissie,' he said, smiling. 'He's turning into a beautiful animal. You're going to make a lot of money selling him at the auction.'

Chrissie beamed. 'Thanks, Dad. You think I'll make enough to buy a good jumping horse?'

'Certainly enough to buy a green one. You might have to train him yourself, but judging from the way you're handling Klutz, I'm sure you'll do fine.' He looked at his watch. 'Well, why don't you finish up with Klutz and then come on in for lunch?'

'Okay,' Chrissie replied. She watched her father leave the barn, then she turned to her horse. 'Do you like attention?' she asked him. 'Well, you've got it. Dr. Anderson thinks you're beautiful, and now you've even managed to charm Dad!' Chrissie smiled and wrapped her arms around Klutz's neck. She realised it was the first time she'd hugged him, and to her surprise, it felt sort of nice.

Klutz nickered.

'But don't let it go to your head, Klutz. The last thing I need is a conceited horse. Just remember you're still kind of funny-looking, and you'll never be as graceful as Outstanding.'

Klutz shook his head from side to side, making Chrissie start laughing all over again. 'What, so you think you're in the same league as Outstanding?' She looked at him as if she were waiting for an answer. 'Oh, terrific! Now I'm arguing with a horse. This is unbelievable.'

Chrissie stepped over to the stall door and peered out to see if anyone was around to hear her. Seeing that the coast was clear, she went back to the colt. 'You know, you may not be graceful, but you're the first horse I've ever met who has a sense of humour.'

After Chrissie had finished grooming Klutz, she put away the brushes and combs and turned

113

to take a last look at him before going in for lunch. For the first time, she tried to look at him with a critical eye, like her father had a few minutes before. He and Dr. Anderson were right. Klutz was no longer as gangly and gawky as he'd been just a few months earlier. He *was* beautiful. His head and neck were fine-boned. His hoofs and legs were delicate but strong. And his dark chestnut coat contrasted beautifully with the white stockings on his four legs. Chrissie smiled and gave him a pat on the nose before leaving the barn.

After lunch, as Chrissie was stacking dirty plates in the sink, her mother came up beside her. 'Chrissie, I have a surprise for you.'

'Oh, really? What is it?' Chrissie said with interest.

'Guess who I talked to just before lunch,' her mother said with a huge grin.

'I don't know. Who?'

'Debbie and her mother, that's who.'

Chrissie looked at Mrs. Williams with surprise. 'Are they moving back here?' she asked excitedly.

'No, dear,' her mother said. 'They're staying right where they are.'

Chrissie's smile faded.

'But the good news is that *you're* not. They called to invite you to spend the last week of

August with them in California. And it's okay with your dad and me.'

'Really?' Chrissie said, her voice rising in excitement.

'Yup. You can go for ten days and return right after Labour Day. The trip is a gift from me and your dad.'

'Wow! That's awesome!' Chrissie yelled, giving her mother a big kiss on the cheek.

'Okay. Now hurry up and finish clearing the table. I'm sure you have more work to do in the barn,' her mother said as she began loading the dishwasher.

When Chrissie finished helping out in the kitchen, she returned to Klutz's stall to take him out to the corral. But as Chrissie led him away from his mother, Teacup whinnied and Klutz suddenly balked.

'What's the matter, Klutz? You've done this a million times before. Why are you suddenly acting up?'

Chrissie tugged on his halter once more, wishing that Teacup hadn't whinnied. Klutz wouldn't have given Chrissie any trouble if he hadn't heard his mother's call. He had done well with the weaning process so far. In fact, he was almost fully weaned. But the colt wouldn't move beyond the stall door.

'I'm sorry, Klutz,' Chrissie finally told him, 'but you've got to get over this.' She knew the situation called for firmness, so she reached for a riding crop hanging on a hook nearby and gave him a little tap on his rear. Klutz instinctively moved away from the unexpected tap and out into the aisle.

'Good boy,' Chrissie said reassuringly. She led Klutz out of the barn and into the corral, and decided that she'd try to teach him how to stand still on command. First she unhooked the lead line attached to his halter, then she positioned him so that he was standing evenly on all four feet and was looking straight ahead.

'Stand!' Chrissie said when she had him in the right position. Then she backed off a couple of feet.

Klutz followed.

'No, Klutz. *Stand* means stand. Don't follow me.' Chrissie tried again, but Klutz just wouldn't stay put.

'Okay! Okay!' Chrissie said. 'Tell you what. If you really want to follow me around, then let's practice leading.' She reattached the lead line to his halter, then started walking in circles and figure eights. They made their way around the corral several times with Klutz walking near her right shoulder.

After a successful half hour of working together, Chrissie decided that it was too hot to work any longer. Klutz pretty much knew how to be led, anyway. He didn't try to rush ahead of her, nor did he lag behind her when they walked.

After she had led the colt out of the corral and over to a big shade tree near the barn, Chrissie sat down under the tree to rest. Soon Klutz began nibbling at the grass under the tree.

'So, Klutz,' Chrissie said. 'Mum said I could go to California to visit Debbie. I just about died when I heard the news. Can you imagine? Me? In California with all those celebrities? I just can't wait to go. And I've missed Debbie so much.'

Klutz gave up trying to chew on a clump of dandelions and pressed his face up against Chrissie's thigh. 'Hey, what gives?' she said, laughing. 'Oh, so you think that if you end up in my lap I'll pay more attention to you, huh? Well, it won't work.'

Chrissie got off the grass and began stroking Klutz's soft, fuzzy muzzle.

Klutz woofed softly, obviously enjoying her touch. 'You like that, don't you?' Chrissie said. He rested his nose right on Chrissie's shoulder, as if waiting to be hugged. 'Oh, you're just a big baby,' she said, wrapping her arms around his neck.

Klutz might have felt a little smothered, because after a while he snorted into her hair and pulled away. 'Ick, Klutz! You should've told me if you wanted me to let go!'

Chrissie sat back down on the grass and played with the end of Klutz's lead line. 'So anyway, boy, I'll be leaving for L.A. before the summer show,' she said. 'That's good, because it would be too depressing to go without Tuskers. I'll just go next year when I have a young jumper of my own. So I guess I'll leave around the twenty-fifth of August and return sometime after September fourth. Boy, Deb and I are going to have a blast!'

Suddenly, Klutz snorted loudly and shook his head from side to side. Chrissie immediately stopped talking. She tilted her head and looked at her horse.

'What's the problem? I'll only be gone—' Chrissie stopped midway through the sentence. 'Wait a minute. You're trying to tell me something, aren't you?'

Chrissie watched Klutz as he looked down and pawed the ground. It was as if he wanted her to stay right there on the farm with him. He didn't want her to go away and visit Debbie.

Groaning loudly, Chrissie rested her head in her hands. This was ridiculous. The long days she was spending with the horses must really be getting to her! A horse couldn't possibly understand what she was saying. But when she looked up at Klutz again, she realised that he really did need her to stick around and take care of him. And besides, Klutz was her responsibility.

Chrissie got up and began rubbing the special place behind Klutz's ears. 'I guess it *would* be selfish if I went to California and left you here by yourself. Who'd take care of you? Who'd exercise and feed you? I can't have some stranger taking care of you.'

That night at dinner, Chrissie didn't eat much because she was too busy trying to figure out how to tell her mother she couldn't go to California. She didn't want to seem ungrateful, but there was no way she could leave Klutz. He wasn't even completely weaned. And because he had balked at the barn earlier that day, Chrissie felt he still needed her help and support.

'So, Chrissie,' her father said cheerfully as he cleared the table, 'I hear your mother told you about the trip. Are you excited about seeing Debbie?'

'Actually, I wanted to talk to you both about that. I really appreciate the offer, but I've decided not to go. It hasn't been that long since I saw her last. I mean, she only just moved out there at the beginning of the summer,' Chrissie said, trying to think up excuses.

Her parents were staring at her with odd expressions on their faces.

Chrissie went on. 'And besides, they probably haven't had a chance to get settled in yet.'

Chrissie's mother stopped rinsing the dishes

and sat down at the table. 'Wait a minute. Did I miss something? Are you the same daughter who was practically doing cartwheels when we talked about this earlier?'

'Oh, Mum. Don't get so dramatic. I just don't think I should go. That's all.'

Chrissie got up and started to leave the kitchen.

'Come back here, Chrissie. Talk to me,' her mother called after her. 'There's got to be more to it than that. What's the problem? What's wrong?'

'All right,' Chrissie said impatiently. 'I don't want to leave Klutz, that's all,' she explained. 'He can't be left alone for that long.'

Her mother raised her eyebrows and looked from Chrissie to her husband and back again. 'You don't want to leave Klutz? That's the problem?'

'Chrissie, honey,' her father said, 'you don't have to worry about that horse. Someone will take over your chores for you. Besides, your mother and I want you to have a little time off at the end of the summer.'

Chrissie just shook her head silently.

'Believe me,' her father continued, 'by the end of next month, you'll be dying for a holiday. It's okay . . . honest. You're working very hard with Klutz. And you deserve a chance to relax before school starts.'

'Sorry,' Chrissie said firmly, 'I've made up my mind. I'm not going to trust just anyone with my horse. Now, I've got to get back to the stable.'

Chrissie knew her parents were staring at her as she left the room. 'I never thought I'd see the day when she'd pick that horse of hers over a chance to see Debbie,' she heard her father say as she closed the door behind her.

The sun was just beginning to set when Chrissie reached Klutz's stall. Her colt left his mother's side, sauntered over to her, and began nuzzling her right front pocket, the one Chrissie always kept treats in. Chrissie lifted Klutz's head up by the halter and looked into his big black eyes.

'You know, you're really something! All you ever do is eat and sleep, eat and sleep, while I work my fingers to the bone,' Chrissie said, teasing Klutz. 'Jeez, all you ever do is push me around and beg for more treats. And you don't even say thank you.' She tried to sound angry, but it seemed as if Klutz could see through her little act.

He butted her with his nose and sent her reeling backwards. Then he walked over and put his soft muzzle against Chrissie's cheek.

'Okay! Okay!' Chrissie said, laughing hard. She reached into her pocket and took out a handful of sugar cubes. 'Here.' She held them out and Klutz quickly gobbled them up.

'All right, the party's over. Time to go to work,' she said.

Chrissie spent the rest of the evening with Klutz. It was after eight o'clock when she finally said to him, 'You're going to have one more walk around the corral before bedtime. Come on, let's go! I want to call Debbie tonight and tell her I can't come for a visit.'

Chrissie walked to the front of the stall and removed Klutz's lead line. She hooked the toggle clamp to Klutz's halter and led the horse out to the corral. After she closed the gate behind them, she walked to the centre of the corral and began leading Klutz in a circle.

'Come on! We'll take it slow tonight, but tomorrow I'm going to make you work off all that extra energy you've got stored up. Now, let's get started. We've got a lot of work to do before dark.'

Ten

'BUT DEBBIE,' CHRISSIE PLEADED INTO THE PHONE, 'YOU just don't understand. I've really fallen in love with him. You haven't seen him in a while. He's really turned into a beautiful horse. I don't even want to sell him at auction anymore.'

Chrissie lay on her stomach, sprawled across her bed. She got up for a second to close her window against the chill October wind and then she lay back down.

'Well, unless you kidnap that horse or buy him, I don't see how you can keep him,' Debbie said. 'Besides, what's the big deal? I'm sure you'll raise other horses after Klutz. And don't you want to buy a jumper with the money you get from selling him? You just said you wouldn't be able to start training Klutz to jump until he's two. That's a whole extra year without a horse to jump.'

Chrissie couldn't believe what she was hearing from her friend. She knew Debbie was still upset about the cancelled visit, but three months had gone by and she was still being sort of mean.

'You know, Chrissie, less than a year ago, all you could talk about was Outstanding. There was no other horse for you. And what happened? You got over him. You know why? Because you live on a horse farm. Chrissie, there are lots more horses where Klutz came from. Get over it already.'

'How can you say that?' Chrissie stammered, unable to control her hurt.

'Oh, gosh, Chrissie, I'm sorry. I shouldn't have said that. I know how much Klutz means to you. Have you talked to David? What does he think you should do?'

Chrissie sniffled before answering. 'Well, he's at college, and the only time I get to talk to him is when he calls home to say he needs some more money or that he can't come home for the weekend for some reason or another. I think he's got a girlfriend up there and doesn't want to be away from her for even one weekend. He'll be coming home for Thanksgiving, though.'

'I just knew he'd be snatched up in a minute. Is he as cute as he was before?'

Chrissie didn't answer. Instead she reached over, took a tissue from the box, and blew her nose. Then she crumpled it up and tossed it into the wastepaper basket.

After a moment Debbie said, 'Okay, let's try to look at this situation logically.' She paused, gathering her thoughts. 'What is it exactly that you want?' she finally said.

'Klutz!' Chrissie replied quickly, feeling a bit confused. 'That's what we've been talking about for the last three weeks, isn't it?'

Debbie ignored Chrissie's reply. 'And how can you keep the horse?'

Chrissie thought for a moment before answering. 'Well, I could buy the horse or my parents could give him to me.'

'Yes,' Debbie quickly jumped in, 'but there isn't a good chance that either one of those things will happen, is there?'

'I guess not,' Chrissie said miserably.

'There's one other possibility, though,' Debbie said. 'You could make sure no one else buys the horse at the auction.'

'How could I do *that*?' Chrissie asked, slightly annoyed. 'Get a list of everyone who'll be there and beg them not to buy Klutz?'

'Well, I didn't say I had the *perfect* plan, did I?' Debbie said, sounding hurt. 'I was just trying to help.'

Just then Chrissie heard her mother calling

her from downstairs. 'Chrissie! Are you still upstairs?'

Chrissie covered the mouthpiece of the phone with her hand before shouting her reply. 'Yes, Mum!'

'Well, come down and get washed up. Dinner's ready'

'I'll be right down!' she yelled back. 'I gotta go. Dinner's ready,' she said into the phone. 'Can I call you later?'

'I don't think that's a good idea,' Debbie replied. 'It's almost four o'clock over here and Mum's taking me to the mall and then out to dinner. We won't be home till at least nine, which is midnight your time.'

'Oh, that's right,' Chrissie said dejectedly. 'Then I guess I'll have to wait till tomorrow to talk to you.'

The two friends said their good-byes and hung up. Then Chrissie quickly went into the bathroom and freshened up before heading downstairs.

'So, how's Klutz doing today?' her father asked when she joined her parents at the table. 'Mr. Patterson thinks that horse should bring top dollar at the auction.'

Chrissie's stomach twisted into a tight knot, and she gathered all her courage before speaking. 'Dad, what do you think about keeping Klutz around for a little while longer?

126

He's the first Anglo-Arab we've raised and . . . uh . . . it would be useful to see how he, you know, progresses. I could train him and we could eventually see if he turns into a good jumper or something.'

Chrissie's parents exchanged looks across the table.

'I don't think that's such a great idea, Chrissie,' her father began. 'He's got to be taken to auction in December.'

'But Dad,' Chrissie said, trying not to whine, 'I don't think we should sell Klutz yet. How about keeping him just until next year?' Chrissie crossed her fingers under the table and hoped that that would sound reasonable.

'Well, now, Chrissie,' her mother said, 'I don't think that would be possible, either.'

'Your mother's right,' her father put in. 'We can't sell a two-year-old at a yearling auction. You know what happened with Outstanding, Chrissie.' He shook his head regretfully at the memory. 'It's such a pity that he won't be eligible for December's yearling auction. Now we'll have to take him to a less profitable auction.'

Chrissie couldn't speak because the lump in her throat seemed to be growing bigger and bigger. She jumped up from her chair and raced out of the room, leaving her bewildered parents sitting at the dinner table.

* * *

For the next week Chrissie continued to spend hours on the phone with Debbie, trying to figure out a viable way to keep Klutz. But no matter how hard they tried, they couldn't come up with any solutions.

Buying Klutz herself seemed to be the only option, though Chrissie suspected she'd never be able to scrape up enough money. The first chance she got, she headed down to the barn to find Mr. Patterson. She had to find out how much money she would need to buy a yearling.

'Mr. Patterson,' she said when she found him, 'do you have a minute?'

'Sure, Chrissie, what can I do for you?'

'Mr. Patterson, *you* know how the yearling auction works. Tell me, how much do you think Klutz will go for at the sale two months from now?'

Mr. Patterson thought for a moment. After scratching his head a couple of times while he did some mental calculations, he replied, 'I don't know. I'd say he might bring in something like five to eight thousand dollars, which means you'll receive somewhere between twenty-five hundred and four thousand dollars.'

'He'd go for that much?' Chrissie said, wide-eyed.

'I think so. Even though he's a new breed for us, we have an outstanding reputation, you know. And who knows? If the market's right, he might even go for more,' he said. 'You're going to get a nice piece of change when that little colt goes on the block.'

Chrissie drew in her breath. She didn't have anywhere near enough money to buy Klutz at the auction if the bidding went that high. In fact, she didn't have enough to buy Klutz if he sold for *half* the price Mr. Patterson was talking about. And it would do no good to tell her parents she'd forfeit the money if she could keep Klutz. She knew exactly what they'd say: 'Our horses aren't pets. They're livestock, raised to be sold.'

'Thanks, Mr. Patterson,' Chrissie said despondently. She turned and walked back toward Klutz's stall.

She talked softly in her horse's ear as she began untangling his mane with the curry comb. 'What a bummer! Now what am I going to do? Just look at the mess you've got me into. Why did you have to be so cute? Why did you have to be so smart? Why did I have to fall in love with you?' she said, sobbing into Klutz's neck.

For the rest of the week Chrissie walked around in a daze. Then one day her father called her into his office. From the look on his face

Chrissie knew something was wrong.

'Chrissie,' her father began sternly, 'this just arrived in the morning mail, and your mother and I want an explanation.' In his hand he held the telephone bill. 'You called Debbie almost every single day for the past month. Did you realise how high the bill would be when you made those calls?'

Chrissie stared down at her shoes. 'No, Dad. I'm sorry.'

'Sorry?' her father replied angrily. 'You ran up a bill for two hundred and thirty-eight dollars and all you have to say for yourself is "sorry"? Well, there are going to be some new rules around here. First, you'll have to pay back the money for this bill and the calls that will appear on next month's bill.' He threw the bill down on his desk. 'You'll take half from your savings and work the rest off doing additional chores around the house. Second, no more long-distance calls to your friends – or anyone else, for that matter – without our permission. Understood?'

'Understood,' Chrissie replied sombrely. 'I'm really sorry, Dad, but it was important for me to talk to Debbie.'

'Chrissie, you chose to cancel your visit to California,' he said, then waited for a response. Chrissie just looked down at the floor.

'Listen,' her father said in a softer voice, 'I

know it's hard to make new friends, but you have to try.'

Chrissie managed a weak smile, but she knew he wouldn't understand even if she tried to explain. All she could think about was rule number one – don't get attached. If her father knew she had violated that rule, he'd take it as a sign of her immaturity, and she had worked too hard to gain his respect to lose it now.

'Thanks, Dad. But I'll be okay.'

'All right. Then this won't happen again?'

'No, I'll stop calling Debbie,' Chrissie said softly.

Her father looked at her affectionately. 'Chrissie, I have an idea. Instead of spending all your time on the phone with Debbie, why don't you just invite her to spend Thanksgiving with us? She's always welcome here, you know. Go call her now and invite her out – you have my permission. Just remember to keep the call short! Say, five minutes. That's one minute for the invitation and four minutes to chat. Does that sound fair?'

Chrissie nodded. She hugged and kissed her father before running out of the room, feeling much better. If Debbie and David both came for Thanksgiving, they could all put their heads together and come up with a plan to keep Klutz!

The next few weeks flew by quickly. With the additional chores she had to do to pay off the phone bill, Chrissie barely had any extra time to spend with Klutz. She also had enough homework to give her grey hair and ulcers. With all those obligations, she didn't have much time to work on a plan to keep her horse, and she still didn't know what she was going to do.

Out of desperation, Chrissie decided to call David . . . collect. If anyone could think of a way to save the horse, David could. It took three tries before Chrissie was able to get him in his room at college.

'Hey, shrimp, this is a surprise. What's up?'

'Not much, Mr. College. I'm adjusting to life without Debbie. That's why I had to call you collect, by the way. I ran up the phone bill calling California and got a warning from you know who.'

David laughed. 'It figures. Don't worry about it. You can call collect anytime. So how's Klutz?'

Chrissie took a deep breath. 'Klutz is actually the real reason I'm calling. David, I need your help.'

'Sure, Chrissie, what is it?'

'David, uh . . . I don't want to sell Klutz at the yearling auction. You've got to help me out. I just don't know what I'm going to do.'

'Chrissie, you seem to be forgetting rule number one.'

'No, I'm not,' Chrissie answered. 'I hate that stupid rule!'

'Okay. Talk,' David said. 'How'd you let yourself get into this mess?'

Chrissie spent the next half hour telling David exactly how she and Klutz had become friends. By the time she finished, she was crying.

'And that's the story,' Chrissie said tearfully. 'So you see, you're my last hope. You just have to help me find a way to keep Klutz.'

David was silent for a long time. 'Look,' he said finally. 'I'll be home in a week for Thanksgiving. We'll try to come up with a solution to your problem then. Okay? Listen, I've got to go. It's getting late and I have to finish a paper.'

'Thanks, David. You're a sweetheart.'

'You bet I am.'

'And thanks for paying for this call. You're the ultimate brother.'

'That goes without saying.'

A few minutes later, Chrissie skipped downstairs. She stopped in the family room to tell her parents, who were watching television, that she was going to say good night to Klutz and then turn in.

As she ran out to the stable she kept thinking about all the good times she would have with Klutz now that David was going to find a way to help her keep him. He had always come through for her in the past. She just knew David wouldn't let her down now that it really mattered.

Eleven

ON THE DAY DEBBIE WAS SUPPOSED TO ARRIVE, Chrissie took extra pains getting Klutz cleaned up and groomed. She wanted him to look perfect for her friend. She spent a lot more time than usual brushing and combing her colt, and she took the time to polish his hooves and tack. Chrissie even braided Klutz's mane and tail, which she had never done before. When she finished with him, she stepped back to admire her work. Klutz looked absolutely beautiful.

'Wow!' Chrissie said to her colt. 'Look at you now! Debbie's going to love you. Who would believe that you were a scrawny, awkward-looking foal just ten months ago? You've turned into such a beauty. Let all those Thoroughbreds eat their hearts out.'

Klutz whinnied and bobbed his head as though he were agreeing with her. Chrissie laughed.

'There's nothing modest about you, is there?' she said. 'Well, you'd better start thinking about thanking the best trainer in the world.'

Klutz snorted loudly.

'Oh, so that's how it's going to be, is it?' Chrissie said, feigning anger. 'I guess I'll just have to show you once and for all who's the boss around here.'

'Oh, really?' Debbie said.

Chrissie nearly jumped on top of Klutz at the sound of her friend's voice. She whirled around and stared at her friend open-mouthed before speaking.

'What are you doing here? Your plane isn't supposed to land for another three hours. We were going to pick you up at the airport.'

'I know, but my mum got me on an earlier flight and your mum decided that we wouldn't tell you about it. Some surprise, huh?'

'The best!' Chrissie gave her friend a big hug, squeezing her as hard as she could.

'Oh, have I got stories to tell you,' Debbie said as she broke free from Chrissie's grasp.

'Me, too,' Chrissie said.

'California is absolutely unbelievable,' Debbie said. Then she began listing the stars she'd seen and the famous places she'd visited.

She was talking as fast as she could, skipping from one story to the next without pausing for air.

Then it was Chrissie's turn, and she began chattering a mile a minute as well. She told Debbie about Klutz and how much he'd changed in ten months. Then she started explaining that while she still hadn't resolved the problem with Klutz, David had promised to come up with a solution.

After about ten minutes of nonstop talking, Klutz came over and nudged Chrissie from behind.

'Oh, you see? This one's already jealous,' Chrissie said, poking him in the nose. Klutz shook his head and snorted. Chrissie looked at Debbie, and they both laughed.

The girls paid attention to Klutz for a few minutes, and then they made a nest for themselves in a pile of hay out in the barn aisle. Chrissie turned to her friend.

'It's hard to believe that you're really here. Five months was such a long time,' she said. 'I thought I'd never see you again.'

'How do you think I felt after you decided not to see me in August?' Debbie said quietly. 'It's still hard for me to deal with this move. I miss you, you know.'

The two girls sat talking quietly as they watched Klutz munch oats from his feed bucket. Every once in a while the colt would prick his ears forward and lift his head as though he were trying to listen in on their conversation.

'He sure has turned into a beautiful animal,' Debbie said. 'No wonder you love him so much.'

'He is beautiful, isn't he?' Chrissie said, bursting with pride.

Then the intercom crackled to life. 'Dinner's being served, girls. Better get up to the house before all the fried chicken's gone!'

'I'll race you!' Chrissie said as she dashed out of the stall with Debbie right behind her.

'No fair!' she hollered at Chrissie. 'I'm your guest. You're supposed to wait for me.'

The two girls exchanged news throughout the whole meal, only stopping to take huge bites of fried chicken, home-fried potatoes, salad, and apple pie.

After they'd eaten and helped clean up, Chrissie and Debbie excused themselves from the table. On their way upstairs, they overheard Chrissie's father say to his wife, 'See? I told you. Chrissie was just moody because she missed Debbie.'

Chrissie looked at Debbie and put her finger to her lips. Once upstairs, the girls unpacked Debbie's clothes and put them away.

'Hey, what's this?' Chrissie said, picking up

a gift-wrapped box on her pillow.

'Let's see,' Debbie said. 'Either you bought yourself a gift, or I must have brought you this. What do you think?'

Chrissie made a face at Debbie as she ripped open the package. Inside was an autographed photo of the rock group Blast and a tape of their newest album.

'Oh, this is great!' Chrissie cried as she bounced up and down on the bed. 'They're my favourite group. Where did you get this? Did you meet them? In person?'

Debbie could hardly contain herself. 'Yes! It was totally awesome! You would have just *died* if you'd been there.'

'Tell me everything!' Chrissie demanded.

'My Mum got the concert tickets from one of her clients, and she took me to see them last week,' Debbie explained. 'We had a V.I.P. backstage pass for after the show, so that's how I got to meet them.'

'Cool! You're so lucky!'

'They gave me a photo, and I asked them if I could have one for you, too,' Debbie went on. 'And they gave it to me! I had to buy the tape at a store, though.'

'I love it,' Chrissie said with a huge smile. 'Thanks so much.'

'Next time they're in town, you should come out and we'll go see them together,'

Debbie said enthusiastically.

'Okay,' Chrissie said, putting the tape away. 'So,' she said, changing the subject, 'you've got to help me come up with a plan to keep Klutz.'

Debbie shrugged. 'Well, I've thought about it, but I haven't come up with anything. I mean, if you can't buy him, then I guess you'll have to accept the fact that he'll be gone next month. But you *can* start getting excited about the new horse you can buy with the money you make.'

'Debbie!' Chrissie shouted. 'What are you saying? Don't you get it? Klutz *can't* be sold.'

'Chrissie, I'm sorry But you can't expect a miracle to happen. I know it's not fair, but why can't you just get used to the idea of letting him go?'

Chrissie had been so happy until just a moment earlier. Now she felt awful. Why couldn't her friend understand? She flung herself on to the bed and buried her face in a pillow.

'Hey, come on. It's not that bad,' Debbie said gently.

'What do you mean? It's terrible,' Chrissie said in a muffled voice.

'If I didn't know better, my feelings would be hurt,' said Debbie. 'I mean, *I'm* here. And we haven't seen each other for months. I know he's important to you, Chrissie, but he's only a horse. Can't you stop thinking about him at least for tonight?'

'What do you mean, he's only a horse?' Chrissie replied as she angrily wiped the tears from her eyes. 'He's my best friend, especially now that Tuskers has been put out to pasture. I talk to him, and he listens. *He* didn't leave me and run off to California.'

'But Chrissie, you know I didn't *want* to move. It was my mother's job. I'm still your best friend. How can you think that I left you behind on purpose?'

'Look, maybe I'm just tired right now. Let's get some sleep,' Chrissie finally said. 'I have to get up early tomorrow morning for Klutz.'

'Yeah, okay,' Debbie replied as she slipped into her sleeping bag. Chrissie reached over and switched off the light before she climbed into bed.

'I'm sorry,' Chrissie whispered in the darkness.

'Me, too,' answered Debbie. 'Hey, maybe David can help you.'

Chrissie rolled on to her back. 'Yeah, I think David will know what to do. He'll think of a way for me to keep Klutz.'

The next thing she knew, Chrissie was hearing her alarm clock go off. She slowly rose from her warm bed and swung her legs over the side.

Then she dragged herself into the bathroom to wash and dress. Fifteen minutes later, she returned to her bedroom and sat on her bed. Debbie was still sleeping.

Maybe I'm being too hard on her. After all, she's never owned a horse before and doesn't really know how close Klutz and I have become, Chrissie thought.

She leaned over her friend. 'Hey! Wake up! Time to go to work!'

'Just ten more minutes, Mum,' Debbie said in her sleep.

Chrissie had to cover her mouth to keep from laughing. 'Debbie, dear,' she said, playing along, 'you have to get up now. You'll be late for school.' She shook her friend awake.

'All right, Mum, I'm up! I'm up!' Debbie flipped the sleeping bag back and sat up. It was only after she'd rubbed the sleep from her eyes that she realised where she was.

'Oh!' she said quickly, blushing in embarrassment.

Chrissie grinned. 'Listen, about last night,' she said. 'I'm really sorry. I shouldn't have said those things to you. I know it's not your fault that you had to move away.'

'Oh, Chrissie, I'm sorry, too. I was being totally insensitive,' Debbie explained. 'I should have understood how much Klutz means to you.'

Chrissie gave her a warm smile and a quick hug. 'Come on. We have to hurry. I want you to help me with my chores this morning so we can spend the afternoon with Lucy and Carla.'

'Great!' Debbie said excitedly. 'Give me five minutes and I'll meet you downstairs.'

Chrissie looked at her friend suspiciously. 'Five minutes? It takes you longer than that just to decide what outfit you're going to wear.'

Debbie grabbed her pillow and flung it at Chrissie. Then Chrissie took her own pillow and hit Debbie on the head before running out of the room. She was still laughing when she got downstairs to the kitchen.

Ten minutes later, Debbie was seated at the table with Chrissie and her parents.

'So, what are you two planning for today?' Chrissie's father asked as he put down his cup of coffee.

'Well, Debbie's going to help me with Klutz this morning, and Carla and Lucy are stopping by after lunch for a little while,' Chrissie answered, popping the last bit of toast in her mouth. 'I thought the four of us could spend some time together and catch up.'

'Sounds like fun,' her mother said. 'But don't forget that David will be arriving sometime late this afternoon.'

After breakfast, Chrissie and Debbie picked up fresh buckets of oats and water before

143

heading for Klutz's stall.

'Hi, boy,' Chrissie said as she walked over to her horse. 'Did you have a good night?'

Klutz snorted and pawed the ground while Chrissie placed a bucket in front of him. Then she poured the water into the trough.

Debbie stood by, watching, and shook her head. 'I can't believe it. It almost seems as if he understands everything you're saying to him.'

Chrissie smiled. 'Believe it,' she said. 'He's a smart guy.'

For the rest of the morning Chrissie and Debbie took care of Klutz. By lunchtime, they'd finished brushing him and cleaning out the stall. Then after lunch, Chrissie finished exercising Klutz while Debbie helped get the dishes cleaned up. By two o'clock, Lucy and Carla had arrived, and the four of them went up to Chrissie's room.

Debbie immediately filled them in about how she'd met the teenage star of television's hottest new show.

' . . . and so when we left the restaurant, he smiled at me. I thought I'd die!'

'Is he as cute in person as he is on TV?' Carla asked. The look in her eyes told the other girls that she had a huge crush on the actor.

'Nope!' Debbie replied quickly.

Carla's eyes opened wide. 'He's not?'

144

'He's even cuter!' Debbie said.

Carla breathed a sigh of relief.

Chrissie was sitting by her dresser, listening to the others chat. When Debbie finished telling another story, Chrissie got up and moved over by her closet. 'Hey, does anybody want to take a ride?' Chrissie asked as she began taking out her riding boots.

'Yeah,' Debbie said. 'Let's go to the shops.'

Chrissie froze. 'I meant horseback riding, not a car ride. We have four horses we can use—'

But the other girls didn't seem to hear her.

'Awesome idea, Debbie,' Lucy said.

'Yeah,' Carla added.

'All right, then,' Debbie said, clapping her hands together. 'Mrs. Williams told me she'd run us over there if we wanted to go today.'

Chrissie was stunned. 'She did? When?'

'Oh, I asked her while I was helping her clean up in the kitchen,' Debbie explained. 'She said she had to go shopping later, and she'd drop us in town on her way. We'll have about an hour there before she picks us up on the way back.'

'But I don't want to go shopping today. I'd just as soon stay here and go horseback riding,' Chrissie said, putting on her boots.

'Are you sure?' Debbie asked.

'Yeah, I'm positive.'

'Okay,' Debbie continued, 'then the three of

us will go. I should be back by four. Your mum said she'd drop Lucy and Carla home on the way back.' She grabbed her coat and bag. 'See you later, Chrissie,' Debbie called over her shoulder as she left, with Lucy and Carla following close behind.

Chrissie plopped down on her bed. How could Debbie just get up and leave? Would she rather go shopping than spend time with her best friend?

When the sound of an approaching car woke her up, Chrissie realised she must have drifted off. A quick glance at her watch told her it was six o'clock – and she hadn't spent any time with the horses at all that afternoon. Jumping off her bed, she looked out the window and saw David's car pull up to the front of the house. Chrissie ran downstairs and found her parents already greeting him. Debbie was there, too. Ignoring them, she ploughed ahead and jumped into David's arms.

'Hey, are you trying to squash me?' David said as he gave his sister a kiss and a hug.

'You know you love it.' Chrissie squeezed her brother's neck as hard as she could.

'Okay! I give up!' David said, laughing as Chrissie continued to cling to his neck. Finally he prised her off, and she let him go upstairs to unpack and get ready for dinner.

Chrissie waited only a few minutes before she followed him upstairs to his room and knocked on the door.

'Come in,' David said.

Chrissie opened the door and walked in. 'Boy, am I glad to see you,' she said as she sat down on his bed.

'I'm glad to see you, too. How's everything going?'

'Well – great, if you've figured out a way for me to keep Klutz.' Then she grabbed her brother by the arm and pulled him to the door. 'Come on. Let me show you how great he looks.'

'Take it easy. I'm coming.' David grabbed his jacket from the bed and slipped it on.

When they got to Klutz's stall, Chrissie's brother became very serious. He looked at the colt thoroughly before saying a word.

'Hey, you weren't kidding,' he finally said. 'He's a beauty! I'm impressed.'

Chrissie was about to explode with pride. She really respected her brother's horse sense, and all this praise for Klutz was making her feel great.

She took a deep breath. 'So, have you figured out a way for me to keep him?' she asked her brother hopefully.

'Gee, I'm sorry, Chrissie. I got so caught up in exams that I haven't given it much thought.'

Chrissie looked at him with a hurt expression. 'Oh,' she said quietly.

'Hey, cheer up. We have four days before I have to go back to college,' David said, trying to sound upbeat. 'Between the two of us, I'm sure we can come up with something. Okay?'

Chrissie returned David's smile. 'Okay. Do your stuff,' she said. 'Let's see if all that money Mum and Dad are throwing away on your education is worth it.'

'Why, you—' David reached down, grabbed a huge handful of straw, and stuffed it down the back of Chrissie's shirt.

'Look out!' Chrissie yelled as she grabbed David around the knees and knocked him down. The two of them tumbled around in the straw, laughing.

'First fall goes to Chrissie Williams!' shouted Chrissie.

'Are you nuts?' David yelled as he tried to prise himself out from under his sister. 'I had you pinned first.'

'Oh yeah?' Chrissie said as she began tickling her brother's stomach. 'Do you want to bet?'

'Hey,' Debbie said breathlessly, running into the barn, 'dinner's ready.'

Chrissie got up and picked the straw off her clothes. 'Come on, race you back to the house. Last one there's a gelding!'

Chrissie took off first, followed closely by David and Debbie, but David soon took the lead and beat the girls to the house.

During dinner David talked nonstop about his classes. Chrissie was glad her brother seemed to be so happy, but all the college talk was boring her. At one point, David was actually trying to convince their father to computerise his business.

'If you computerise the farm, you'd be able to do a whole month's worth of tasks in a couple of hours,' David said enthusiastically. 'Inventory, purchases, bookkeeping, even the different mixes you use to feed the horses could be put on the computer. Then all you'd have to do is print out the information.'

'Really? Well, I'm certainly glad we've managed to hold on to this little farm for almost a hundred years until you could get us computerised,' Chrissie's father said with a grin.

'By computerising, you'd certainly speed up productivity with a minimal investment.'

'Your brother's so smart,' Debbie whispered to Chrissie.

Chrissie rolled her eyes. She couldn't believe that Debbie still had a thing for her brother.

'So, David, what are you doing after dinner tonight?' Chrissie's mother asked.

'Well,' David said, 'a bunch of us decided that

149

we'd get together over at Karen Moffett's. We're going to listen to some music and stuff. But don't worry, I won't stay out too late.'

'All right, but don't forget you have to help set up for tomorrow's dinner,' she said.

'No problem. Everything will get done in plenty of time.'

'Hey, what about us?' Chrissie said to no one in particular. 'What are we supposed to do?'

'Oh, I have plans for you two,' her mother answered. 'First you're going to help me bake all the pies for tomorrow's feast, and then you're going to help me eat a large bowl of popcorn while we watch some movies your father picked up at the video store.'

Chrissie looked at Debbie and shrugged. She had hoped that they could do something exciting . . . like maybe spend the evening in the stall with Klutz. But she knew it would be useless to argue with her parents. And besides, baking dessert and watching videos wouldn't be too bad.

Later, as David was leaving for the evening, Chrissie stopped him at the door. 'I thought you were going to help me with Klutz,' she said.

'I will, but not tonight.' David smiled at her. 'See you later.'

'But David—' Chrissie began.

'We'll talk tomorrow, Chrissie. Good night.' David opened the door and walked out.

Chrissie and Debbie stood on the porch and watched him drive off.

'Let's go help your mum now,' Debbie said in an effort to distract Chrissie from thinking about Klutz.

'I'll be right in,' Chrissie told her.

'Uh, Chrissie,' Debbie said uncertainly, 'I'm really sorry about taking off with Carla and Lucy this afternoon. I didn't mean to make you feel bad.'

'I know. Don't worry about it.' Chrissie smiled at her friend, then watched her turn towards the kitchen.

As soon as Debbie was gone, Chrissie felt her spirits deflate. There was nothing she could do to help Klutz. No one was coming up with a solution to the problem because there *was* no solution.

She took a deep breath and started to go into the kitchen, but then she suddenly changed direction and ran out towards the barn.

When she felt safe and secure in her horse's stall, Chrissie started to sob. 'Why can't anyone help me?' she lamented. 'How come you're the only one who understands me?'

Chrissie slumped down next to her horse and looked up into his eyes. 'But even you don't know what I'm going through,' she told him.

Klutz snorted in response, but Chrissie didn't find his reply very satisfying.

'Yeah, I know. This really *is* a tough one. But you can trust me, boy. I'm working on it night and day. I'll keep you, no matter what it takes!'

Twelve

CHRISSIE WAS SILENT DURING THE LONG CAR RIDE HOME from the airport. She and her mother had just dropped Debbie off for her flight back to California, and Chrissie was still depressed about selling Klutz at the yearling auction. Though she tried to get excited about buying a jumper with the money from Klutz's sale, she wasn't having much luck. She knew that she could train almost any horse to jump, and the horse she wanted to work with, the horse she already loved, was Klutz.

This was the worst Thanksgiving I've ever had! Chrissie thought as she watched the road signs go by. *Why couldn't Debbie and David have spent more time helping me come up with a way to keep Klutz? If only David hadn't had to work around the farm during the day and hadn't run off every night to some party ...*

She had tried to get her brother to sit down and talk to her before the big Thanksgiving dinner, but he had had too many things to do, and her mother had been constantly calling on Chrissie to help out, too.

'I'm sorry, Chrissie. But Mum needs me to set up the tables and chairs before the guests arrive,' David had said. 'Maybe we'll be able to sneak off to a corner before I go over to Jason's tonight. Okay?'

What else could Chrissie have said but okay? Then dinner had run longer than expected, and David had left even before it was over, so she never got a chance to talk to him that evening.

Friday and Saturday had been no better. David had had work to do around the farm, helping their father repair the tack and exercise the horses. And in the evenings he had gone out with his friends. Chrissie had tried to catch him before he left to go back to school that morning, but first he'd had to load the car, and then he was gone.

Debbie had been even less help than David. And not only that – Chrissie had discovered that Debbie had turned into a drip since she'd moved to California. 'Gee, isn't David cute?' she had whispered to Chrissie every time she saw him. She would even stare moon-eyed at David at the table during meals.

And when Debbie wasn't trying to get his attention, she was going on about her cool friends in Los Angeles and how much fun she had living out there. The more she'd talked, the more alone Chrissie had felt.

Chrissie had asked her so-called best friend to do stuff with her several times. 'Hey, Debs, do you want to go horseback riding or help me with Klutz?' Chrissie had suggested every day Debbie was there. But Debbie had said either 'No thanks, maybe later' or 'No, but I'd sure like to go to town.'

When the car finally pulled up to the front of the house, Chrissie jumped out and ran up to her room before her mother could stop her. She dropped her coat on to the floor and flung herself on to the bed.

For the next hour, Chrissie sobbed her heart out under the covers. Then, just as suddenly as the outburst started, it ended. She quickly sat up, took a deep breath, and wiped her tear-streaked face on her sleeve. She knew that the only thing that would make her feel better was to see Klutz.

She put her coat back on and walked over to the barn. Before entering her colt's stall, she grabbed a handful of carrots from the bucket.

'I would have been better off spending all my time with you,' Chrissie said as her horse munched on the carrots. 'At least I'd know that we spent as much time as possible together before we had to say good-bye.'

Chrissie walked over to the corner of the stall and sat down on a bale of hay. Klutz followed and nudged her with his muzzle.

'What?' Chrissie said sadly.

Klutz nudged her again a little harder.

Chrissie tried pushing the horse away, but the colt refused to leave her alone. A third, even stronger nudge sent Chrissie straight into the hay.

Chrissie looked up at Klutz and burst into giggles, and before long she was rolling around on the floor of the stall, laughing and throwing handfuls of hay at her horse. Klutz whinnied as though to say, 'See? It's not so bad.'

Soon Chrissie rose to her feet and gave him a big hug. 'Thanks,' she said to the horse. 'I really needed that. You go to sleep now and I'll see you in the morning. Okay?' She scratched Klutz behind the ears for a few minutes before she left the stall and returned to the house.

The next morning, as Chrissie was eating breakfast, her father joined her at the table. 'Don't forget to come right home after school today,' he said. 'Dr. Anderson's coming over to check out the pregnant mares and weanlings we'll be showing at the auction. I'll be needing your help.'

Chrissie felt her face grow pale and her heart

begin to race at the mention of the auction, but she wasn't going to let her parents know how upset she was at the thought of losing Klutz. *I have to be brave*, she told herself. *I have to show them that I can handle this.*

'Are you okay?' her mother asked her, touching a hand to Chrissie's forehead.

Chrissie didn't respond.

'Chrissie! Are you okay?' Mrs. Williams repeated.

'Sure, Mum,' she said, a little too quickly. 'I was just thinking about all the things I have to do.'

A few minutes later, Chrissie excused herself from the table and went up to her room. *They'll never take Klutz away from me!* Chrissie resolved as she took the stairs two at a time. *I just can't let it happen!*

In a daze, Chrissie floated through her first day back at school after the holiday. All through her classes, she couldn't think about anything but Klutz. Before she knew it, she was getting off the school bus in the late afternoon sun and walking back up the driveway to the farm.

She changed out of her school clothes into jeans, paddock boots, a sweatshirt, and a jacket and went to find Dr. Anderson at the stables. As she closed the barn door behind her, Chrissie saw Dr. Anderson emerging from one of the stalls.

'Hi, Chrissie,' the doctor called out. 'How's my future partner doing?'

'I'm okay,' Chrissie said, approaching her. 'Have you examined Klutz yet?'

'Nope,' the veterinarian replied. 'I thought I'd wait for you before checking out the yearling that will be the star attraction at the upcoming auction.'

Chrissie looked around the barn to make sure the two of them were alone. 'Doc, can I ask you a question?' she said, seeing that there was nobody else around.

'Sure. What is it?'

'Ah . . . can we talk confidentially?' Chrissie said nervously.

Dr. Anderson looked at her with concern. 'Of course we can. What's the matter?'

'Well,' Chrissie began, 'I don't want to give up Klutz. I mean . . .' She hesitated. 'I mean, I don't want him to be sold at the auction. I want to keep him.'

'Come over here and sit down, Chrissie,' the vet said gently. She led the way to some bales of hay in the corner of the barn and sat down. Then she motioned for Chrissie to sit next to her.

Chrissie looked at the sad smile on Dr. Anderson's face and lowered her eyes.

'Chrissie, why don't you talk to your folks about this?' Dr. Anderson asked, gently tilting Chrissie's face up with a finger under her chin. 'Maybe they'll let you keep him. Or maybe they'll let you buy him.'

'No,' Chrissie answered, shaking her head. 'That won't work. You know their rule about not getting involved with the livestock.'

'Well, you have every reason to be sad,' Dr. Anderson said. 'I know exactly what you're going through. It's tough to have to give up something you love.'

'I really don't see why my folks have to sell Klutz,' Chrissie said. 'He's just another horse to them, but to me he's everything.'

'I know. It doesn't seem fair, does it?' Dr. Anderson said. 'But I'm sure things will work out. And listen, if I figure out a way to help you keep him, I'll let you know right away. All right?'

'All right,' Chrissie replied, already beginning to feel a little more hopeful.

'Well, time to go back to work now.' Dr. Anderson rose and started toward Klutz's stall.

Chrissie slowly got up and followed. She wanted to believe what the vet was saying, but she didn't feel totally convinced.

How can things possibly work out? Chrissie wondered. *After I lose Klutz, nothing will ever be the same again!*

Thirty minutes later, the doctor put her stethoscope away and closed up her bag. 'Chrissie, you should be proud to know that this is one of the finest Anglo-Arabs I've ever seen. Klutz is in peak condition.'

Chrissie beamed at the praise in spite of her misery.

'I have to finish inspecting the other weanlings now,' the doctor said. 'I'll see you before I leave. Okay?'

Chrissie nodded. Then she went over to the wall just outside Klutz's stall and took his lead line and a driving whip. She attached the line to the colt's halter and led the horse out of the stall.

By the time she got outside, it was dark. She led Klutz into the corral and replaced his lead line with a longe line. Then, holding the line in her right hand and the whip in her left, Chrissie began putting Klutz through his paces.

First she walked him briskly. After a few minutes, she decided to pick up the pace. 'Trot!' she said as she snapped the whip behind her horse. Klutz immediately began to trot in a clockwise circle, and not once did he stray off his course. After a couple of minutes, Chrissie slowed Klutz to a walk, then started the whole exercise again, this time going counter-clockwise.

'Good boy!' Chrissie said when she had

160

finished trotting him. 'You're doing so well today. You haven't run at me even once. Should we try to canter now, boy?' she asked uncertainly. 'Think you can handle that?'

Chrissie had never tried cantering him before, because she knew it takes a lot of strength to control a young horse who's learning to canter on a longe line.

'Okay, here we go,' Chrissie said under her breath.

She started trotting Klutz again. After a few minutes, Chrissie picked up the pace and snapped the whip. 'All right, Klutz, canter!' she commanded.

Klutz went straight into a fluid canter. Chrissie was thrilled to watch him. He was so graceful at the end of the longe line, picking up speed with each stride. His muscles bunched up with the effort of every movement, and he looked powerful and elegant. He went around and around, faster and faster. Then suddenly King, the Williamses' dog, ran into the ring and started to bark.

Frightened, Klutz reared, wrenching the line out of Chrissie's hand. She was thrown to the ground.

Fortunately, Chrissie's father and Dr. Anderson were just leaving the foaling and yearling barn. Hearing the commotion, the two raced to the corral. They found Chrissie

161

sprawled on the ground with a frightened horse rearing up near her. Her father swiftly leaped over the corral fence and pulled Chrissie out of the way just as Klutz's hoofs came crashing down.

'Wow! That was close!' her father said when he caught his breath. 'Are you all right?'

Chrissie just barely nodded. Her left arm and shoulder were already beginning to throb.

Dr. Anderson calmed Klutz down while Chrissie tried to explain to her father what had happened.

'Chrissie, you know you shouldn't have been cantering Klutz. You and Klutz could have got seriously injured. I can't believe you tried something as stupid as that! I don't want you doing that again without my permission. Is that clear?'

'Yes, sir,' Chrissie replied meekly.

'In fact, I think it might be a good idea if we got one of the grooms to exercise Klutz from now on. I don't want to take a chance on you getting hurt.'

'Oh, Dad!' Chrissie cried out. 'Don't take Klutz away from me. I know I can take care of him without any help. Honest! And it was King's fault, not mine. Klutz was doing great until that dumb dog started barking. This won't happen again. I promise!'

'Don't worry, Chrissie,' he said, completely

162

misunderstanding her distress. 'You'll still get the money from Klutz's sale.'

'Dad,' Chrissie cried, 'that's not the point. I don't care about the money! Please don't take him away from me sooner than you have to. I know I have to sell him, but please let me work with him until then. *Please!*'

'Well . . . he's getting bigger and stronger every day, Chrissie. It might be too difficult for you—'

'Come on, Dad. Please?' Chrissie begged.

'All right,' her father conceded reluctantly. 'I'll give you one more chance. But if this happens again, I'll get someone else to exercise your colt.'

'Okay.' Chrissie breathed a huge sigh of relief.

Dr. Anderson finished checking Klutz for injuries, then she turned to Chrissie. 'Well, your horse looks fine. He was just a little spooked,' she said.

'I'd better go put him back in his stall,' Chrissie said, taking the lead line from Dr. Anderson. 'Thanks.'

When Chrissie had Klutz back in his stall and had wiped him down, she began stroking his muzzle. 'You heard my father. Now please, don't do that again. I don't want anyone else working with you. We . . . we may not have much longer together,' she managed to get out. 'And I don't want to say good-bye to you before I have to.'

Klutz whickered and rubbed his nose against Chrissie's cheek.

'Good! I knew you'd understand.' Chrissie gave the colt a handful of chopped apple to eat. 'See you tomorrow, boy,' she said as she patted his muzzle and kissed him. 'Our three weeks together will be worth all the years we're going to miss. I love you, Klutz. You're my Klutz and only mine, no matter who ends up buying you. Good night . . . until tomorrow.'

Thirteen

AS CHRISSE LED KLUTZ BACK TO HIS STALL AFTER A workout three weeks later, she couldn't help but feel very unhappy. In less than twenty-four hours her horse would be sold. She felt a lump begin to rise in her throat, but she managed to fight back the tears. Since the incident with King in the corral, she'd been spending every free moment with Klutz, trying to make the most of the time they had left together. But now their time had almost run out.

'Oh, Klutz!' she cried. 'What am I going to do when you're gone? I'm going to miss you so much.'

Once in his stall, Klutz began pawing at the straw on the floor, a sign that he was ready for a treat. Chrissie smiled as she reached into her pocket and pulled out a handful of carrots, which the colt immediately devoured.

Chrissie stroked his mane and neck. She knew he liked her to do that while he ate, and Chrissie had made up her mind that, for the little time he had left at Williams Farm, she would do all his favourite things.

'Hey, how would you like some company tonight?' she said as he finished the last bite of carrot and walked over to his water bucket. 'I'll sleep here in the stall with you, if you like. I'm sure Mum and Dad will say it's okay. Especially since I have to get up early in the morning to get you ready... for the auction.'

Klutz whinnied his agreement.

'You like the idea? I'll run up to the house and get a couple of blankets and a pillow. Be right back.' Chrissie turned and raced out of the stall.

In less than five minutes she had gathered the bedding and was on her way back to Klutz's stall. She'd stopped off at her father's office to tell him she was spending the night with Klutz. She knew he'd say it was all right to be with her horse for his last night on the farm, because David had done the same thing five years earlier, on his last night with Gallant Boy.

'I'll tell your mother where you are,' he said. 'Do you need anything?'

Chrissie smiled as bravely as she could. 'No thanks,' she said. But in her thoughts, she added, *Just let me keep my horse.*

Once in the stall, Chrissie quickly spread out one blanket on a bed of clean straw. Then she put her pillow down and covered herself with the other blanket. She lay down, wondering if she would ever get to sleep. At that moment, she felt a sadness so deep that there was no way she could rest.

She recalled how excited she had been the first time she'd ever spent the night in the barn. That had been Christmas Eve, the night Outstanding was born. It seemed so long ago to her now. She had still had so many illusions back then. She'd thought that Outstanding was the most perfect horse in the world, and she'd felt as if his birth was going to change her life. Since then, Chrissie had had so many setbacks and disappointments . . . but she'd also spent nearly a wonderful year with Klutz. Now, when she looked back on that Christmas Eve, Chrissie realised how much she had learned and how much she had accomplished.

'Chrissie, wake up! It's three o'clock. You have to be ready to load the horses in an hour.'

At first Chrissie thought she was dreaming, but when she felt a hand shake her shoulder, she slowly opened her eyes. David stood over her. He must have come home late the night before, and Chrissie was so glad he was there.

When she was on her feet, Chrissie stretched and tried to get the kinks out of her body. She yawned as David picked some straw out of her hair.

'Mum has breakfast ready. If you want to eat, you'd better come on up to the house now.' David turned to head back to the house.

'I'll be there in a minute.' Chrissie wanted some time alone with Klutz before the commotion of the auction began.

David shrugged and walked out of the barn.

'How are you doing, boy?' she asked Klutz.

Klutz came over to get the place behind his ears scratched, and Chrissie was happy to oblige. 'Don't forget, sweetheart, that you'll always be mine in my heart, no matter where you end up.' She looked at him for a long time before turning to leave. 'I'll be back after breakfast,' she said as she let herself out of the stall.

Twenty minutes later Chrissie was brushing her colt for what would be the last time. She had given herself strict orders not to cry, but she couldn't help herself. Even Klutz appeared to be sad, as though he could sense they would soon be separated.

'I'm sure you'll go to a really good place with people who love you,' Chrissie said, choking on the words. She ran the curry comb through Klutz's mane, trying to talk to him through her falling tears.

Finally, unable to take it anymore, she threw the comb on the floor and buried her face in his neck, crying uncontrollably.

'Hey, it's all right, Chrissie. Come on, sis,' she heard her brother say quietly. He entered the stall and walked over to her. He put his arm around Chrissie and led her to the bale of hay in the corner of Klutz's stall. Then he wrapped her in his arms.

'I know how much you're going to miss your colt, but you're not doing yourself or Klutz any good, you know. Now, dry your eyes,' he said, handing her his handkerchief, 'and blow your nose. I understand how you feel, Chrissie, but you don't want Mum and Dad to see you like this. Don't you want them to think you can behave like a responsible adult?'

Chrissie knew her brother was right. She dried her eyes and blew her nose before giving her brother back his handkerchief.

David looked at the damp rag. 'Gee. Thanks a lot!'

Chrissie couldn't manage even the smallest smile, so she hooked up Klutz's lead line to his halter. She took a deep breath and sadly led her colt out of his stall for the last time.

The two large horse vans were parked right outside the weanling stable. One by one, the grooms and hired hands were leading the colts and fillies that were going to auction up the

169

ramps and into the vans.

Each van was capable of holding up to eight horses or ten yearlings. The interior walls were heavily padded from floor to ceiling to protect the horses during the ride. A thick layer of straw was placed on the floor of the van for comfort. Hanging from the wall in each of the portable stalls were individual feed and water buckets.

It took over an hour to load each van, because the horses had to be properly loaded and tied. The sun still hadn't come up yet when the two vans, Mr. Patterson's pickup truck, and the Williamses' jeep pulled out of the driveway to begin the hour-and-a-half drive to the auction.

At seven fifteen the Williams Farm convoy pulled up at the Chester Grange Arena, and less than an hour later all their horses had been off loaded and put in the temporary corral assigned to them.

As soon as things had settled down, Chrissie's father closed the corral gate and walked over to Chrissie and David. 'David, go find out from Mr. Bryant what time we're scheduled to show our horses. He should be over in the office.'

'Okay, Dad. Mind if I take Chrissie with me?'

'Good idea. Here,' Mr. Williams said, taking a twenty-dollar bill from his pocket. 'Why don't you bring back some coffee and doughnuts for everyone, too? This should cover it.'

David took the money and draped his arm

170

around his sister's shoulder.

'Come on, shrimp, I'll buy you breakfast.'

Chrissie looked up into her brother's eyes and tried to smile, but she was sure her attempt was pretty pathetic.

Mr. Bryant, the man in charge of the auction, was just coming out of his office when David and Chrissie got there. He'd known the Williams family for more than twenty-five years.

'Why, hello, David, Chrissie,' Mr. Bryant said as he shook hands with both of them. 'How's the family? Boy, I can't get over how big the two of you have grown since last year's auction.'

'Everyone's fine, thanks. Dad wants to know what time we're scheduled to show,' David said.

Mr. Bryant checked the schedule on his clipboard before replying. 'You're on right after Jeffries Farm. That should be around nine thirty. I'll stop by to see your folks later.'

'Okay, Mr. Bryant,' David replied. 'Thanks. Come on, Chrissie. Let's get some food.'

Chrissie helped David carry trays of coffee and doughnuts back to the Williamses' holding corral. After relaying Mr. Bryant's message to their parents, Chrissie and David grabbed some doughnuts and sat down to eat.

Chrissie took two bites of a doughnut, but

couldn't eat any more. A feeling of dread had descended on her. Klutz would be lost without her, and she would be lost without him. But there was nothing she could do to stop the disaster from happening. She got up, walked over to the corral, and looked at the horses they'd brought to the auction. There, in the far corner, stood Klutz.

When Klutz saw her, he came over and put his head over the corral fence. Chrissie began stroking the colt's mane. Then she scratched behind his ears, all the while talking to him quietly. She had no idea how long she'd been standing there when David called her name.

'Come on, Chrissie. We're up next.'

That was enough to snap her out of it. Like a robot, she walked into the corral carrying Klutz's lead line. She hooked it to his halter mechanically, then led him out of the corral.

Chrissie didn't remember much of what happened next. She heard the announcement over the public address system that Williams Farm was up, and she heard Klutz's name announced. She must have somehow led her colt into the arena, because the next thing she knew she was running as fast as she could towards the horse vans. Someone must have led Klutz away from her. And now he was gone forever and the world was just a blur of sounds and movement surrounding her.

Then it was dark outside. Chrissie was lying on the back seat of the jeep and someone had covered her with a blanket. She hoped it was all a dream, a really awful dream. She hoped she'd wake up at home in her bed, and Klutz would be in his stall waiting for her, like always.

Chrissie sat up and saw that her mother was driving and that they were just pulling off the interstate at Middletown. She saw the horse vans in front of them. They were empty

Devastated, Chrissie realised that Klutz really was gone. He was someone else's horse now. Not hers. She'd never see him again. Ever! She had nothing, and she felt that she might never be able to look at another horse again. Chrissie swore to herself that she'd never get close to anything or anyone again. This would be the last time she'd ever lose a friend.

Fourteen

EVEN THOUGH THE NEXT DAY WAS SUNDAY, CHRISSIE'S father called her into his office and gave her a check for thirty-two hundred dollars. Chrissie took it, then looked at it blankly.

'Chrissie,' he said gently, 'would you like to talk about it?'

'Oh, Daddy, I'm so miserable,' she said.

'Try thinking about the jumper you're going to buy. We can go looking for it next weekend, okay?' he said to her gently. Then he looked at Chrissie's crestfallen face. 'Chrissie, I'm sorry you're feeling so bad. But don't worry. Things will start looking up again.'

She nodded, and though she didn't have much energy, made herself speak. 'I don't think I want another horse, Dad. I don't think I could take it. I didn't plan on feeling this way. But I don't know what happened. One minute he was just a way to make money, and the next he was my best friend. Honest, Dad, I tried! I didn't want to love him, but I couldn't help myself.'

With that, Chrissie ran out of the office and went upstairs to her room. She stayed there all day. Her parents and David tried to make things easier for her, but nothing, not even Debbie's call later that night, was able to lift her spirits.

A week later, her mother dragged her to the town so they could finish their Christmas shopping. There hadn't been any time before the auction to do much shopping, so they'd had to leave it to the very last minute. It was already the twenty-fourth of December and Chrissie still had to get gifts for David, Mr. Patterson, Dr. Anderson, and her father.

For three hours, she and her mother fought their way through the crowd of other desperate, last-minute shoppers until they had finally picked out their last present.

'How about stopping for lunch and an ice-cream sundae before we head for home?' her mother asked after they paid for their purchases.

'Whatever you want to do is fine with me,' Chrissie replied noncommittally.

'Listen, we're going to have fun today if it kills us,' her mother said. Then she grabbed

175

Chrissie's arm and dragged her to a restaurant, where she ordered two hamburgers, an order of fries, a Coke for Chrissie and coffee for herself, and two hot-fudge sundaes for dessert.

By the time the meal was over, Chrissie was feeling a little better. But as they were leaving the mall, Chrissie ran into Carla and Lucy. Because of all the time she had been spending with Klutz lately, Chrissie hadn't seen her friends since Thanksgiving.

'Merry Christmas, Mrs. Williams,' the two girls said simultaneously. 'Merry Christmas, Chrissie.'

'Merry Christmas, girls,' Chrissie's mother echoed.

'So how's your horse, Chrissie? Aren't you supposed to be selling him soon? Boy, I'd love to be able to make money like that,' Carla said.

'I sold him yesterday. And his name was Klutz,' Chrissie said, trying to control her quivering voice. 'Come on, Mum. Let's go.' Chrissie turned away and took off without saying another word to her two friends.

When they got home, Chrissie placed her packages under the Christmas tree and then ran out to Klutz's stall. Everything was exactly as she'd left it two days earlier. She sat down on the bale of hay and stared at the ground. She could still hear Klutz snorting and pawing the ground the way he always did when he wanted something from her. To make matters worse, she could still smell him, too.

Chrissie didn't know how long she sat there, but it was dark when she slowly got up and wandered back to the house. For the first time since the auction, she felt hungry enough to sit down at the table and eat a meal.

That night, the Pattersons and the grooms attended the Williamses' traditional Christmas Eve dinner. In spite of her own preoccupations, Chrissie noticed that it was an unusually quiet dinner.

Right after eating, everyone went into the family room. David had a beautiful fire going in the fireplace. Chrissie's mother began playing Christmas carols on the piano and everyone joined in the singing, except Chrissie.

Without anyone seeing her, Chrissie managed to slip out of the room and go upstairs to her bedroom. *She* certainly didn't have any reason to celebrate this Christmas. She fell across her bed, and before she even realised what was happening, she was soon fast asleep.

'Merry Christmas!' David yelled as he barged into her room early the next morning. 'Merry Christmas!'

'What?' she said, still half asleep.

'Come on, sleepyhead. It's time to get up. Everyone's already downstairs in the family room. We're waiting for you so we can open up all the presents.'

'Let me go back to sleep,' she said, moaning as she tried to roll over and pull the covers up over her head. 'You can go and open them without me. I don't care. I don't want anything. Just let me sleep.'

'Sorry, shrimp,' David said. He reached down and grabbed his sister, still wearing her pyjamas, and wrapped her in her blanket. Then he lifted her up off the bed, slung her over his shoulder, and carried her downstairs.

'Put me down!' she yelled. 'You just wait till I get loose. You'll be sorry!'

David didn't say anything to her until he walked into the family room. 'Well, here she is, everyone. Of course, you can see how eager she is to join the family and all of our friends on this most joyous occasion.' David dropped her unceremoniously on the couch and quickly moved away from her. Even though she was still more than a head shorter than he was, she could kick like a mule.

'Come over here, Chrissie, and sit next to me,' her father said.

Chrissie got off the couch with her blanket wrapped around her and reluctantly walked over to her father, who was sitting on the floor. She plunked herself down next to him.

'Go ahead, David,' his mother said. 'You can

178

start handing out the presents now.'

Chrissie loved getting presents, and in spite of herself, she was beginning to get into the spirit of the holiday.

'Chrissie, here's one for you.' David handed her a large box, then picked up two more. 'And here's one for you, Mum, and one for you, Mr. Patterson.'

Before long, all the gifts had been handed out. Chrissie was seated on the floor in the middle of a huge pile of much-needed clothes from her parents, David, and the Pattersons. She had also received a beautiful painting of wild horses from Dr. Anderson and a thin gold bracelet from Debbie. As everyone pitched in to clean up the wrapping paper, ribbon, and empty boxes, her father smiled and turned to her.

'Chrissie, I think there's a box over there we missed. You'd better go see who it's for.'

Chrissie looked in the direction her father was pointing. In the corner of the room was a very large box wrapped in green paper. She went over to it and tried to pick it up, but it was a lot heavier than it looked. Then she checked the card on top. It said, *Merry Christmas, Chrissie.*

'Hey, it's for me,' Chrissie said in a surprised voice as she looked at her parents.

'Well, you might as well go ahead and open it, then,' David said.

Chrissie pulled off the card and opened it.

Inside was an inscription. *To Chrissie. May you use this happily for many, many years to come. You really deserve it.* It was signed by all the grooms, the hands, and the Pattersons.

She looked at all of them with a puzzled expression and began unwrapping the box. Inside was a brand-new Wintec saddle with a shiny nameplate on the back that was ready to be engraved with a horse's name.

'This is so beautiful,' she exclaimed. 'Thank you all very much.'

'Uh, Chrissie,' her father said as she was admiring the saddle, 'I think there's one more gift you didn't open.'

Chrissie looked around the room, but didn't see anything. 'Where?'

'Put your boots and coat on and follow us,' her mother said, leading the way out of the room. 'And hurry!' she called back over her shoulder.

Chrissie ran upstairs and struggled into her paddock boots. She threw her coat on over her pyjamas and raced downstairs after the others.

'Wait up!' she called out, but nobody would slow down for her.

David led the way down to the yearling corral.

There, in the middle of the corral, wearing a large red bow around his neck, stood Klutz.

Everyone was smiling as Chrissie gaped in

disbelief. Then she ran into the corral, threw her arms around his neck, and kissed him. Klutz looked just as happy to see her, and he whinnied in excitement.

'But – but you sold him. I was there,' she finally managed to stammer.

'Chrissie,' her father said as he put his arm around her shoulders, 'the idea came from your brother, Debbie, and Dr. Anderson. They suggested we bid on Klutz ourselves at the auction and give him to you.'

Chrissie stared at him.

'We all saw how much you'd grown as a person during the eleven months you had Klutz, and we're very proud of you,' her mother explained. 'You really learned a lot from this horse. And we think he learned a lot from you, too. Now, how could we break up a winning team like that?'

'But you sold him. I know somebody paid sixty-four hundred dollars for him because you gave me the cheque,' Chrissie replied.

'Do you remember when we spoke to Mr. Bryant at the auction?' David piped up.

'Yes.'

'Well, I slipped him a note Dad had written asking him to stop by as soon as I had you busy with the coffee and doughnuts.'

'That's right,' her father put in. 'Bill Bryant bought Klutz and held him for us until David and I could go pick him up to make your Christmas wish come true.'

'You *will* have to give back the money from the sale, though,' her mother interjected. 'That means no jumper this year. And you know that Klutz is a few years away from being ready to go into the ring, but if you're willing to take a chance on him, we're willing to take a chance on you. Deal?'

'You did all this for me? I . . . I don't know what to say. This is the best present anyone could ever give me. You've given me back . . .' Chrissie's voice trailed off as tears began to run down her face. 'You've given me back my best friend!'

Chrissie threw her arms around her horse's neck. Klutz whinnied and bobbed his head up and down.

'Well,' Mr. Williams said, 'it looks like Klutz agrees, too.'

Then Chrissie started kissing her horse over and over again. Klutz began to paw the ground frantically, and Chrissie felt a surge of joy inside her. 'Of course you agree. You're the smartest, most wonderful Christmas colt in the world!'

**Don't miss the other exciting stories in the
ROSETTES series:**

* * *

Also in the ROSETTES series:

STAR OF SHADOWBROOK FARM
Joanna Campbell

Can Susan ever ride again?

Susan has fallen off horses before. After all, she's been
riding since she was young. But this last spill was
different. Susan only broke her wrist, but she knows it
could have been a lot worse for her or the horse. And it
was her own fault. Now just thinking about riding
terrifies her.

Then Evening Star comes to the horse farm where Susan
lives. Star's elegant gait and graceful stride show he
could become a champion jumper. But he was
mistreated by his former owner, and as a result he trusts
no one in the stable – except Susan. Susan knows only
she can make Star a winner, but she also knows she
isn't ready to ride again . . .

BELL STREET SCHOOL
Holly Tate

1 – WHO'S THAT GIRL?

When Becky Burns arrives at Bell Street School on her first day, she is terrified. Will she like it? Will they like her? And even more important, will they find out the secret of her past? But all her new girl nerves are swept away when it's announced that heart-throb superstar Rory Todd is coming to Bell Street to film his new video – and he wants some kids to appear! Becky is desperate to be one of the chosen few – but so is everyone else . . .